Home for the Holidays

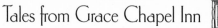 Tales from Grace Chapel Inn

Home
for the
Holidays

REBECCA KELLY

Guideposts
New York, New York

Home for the Holidays

ISBN-13: 978-0-8249-4786-6

Published by Guideposts
16 East 34th Street
New York, New York 10016
www.guideposts.com

Distributed by Ideals Publications, a division of Guideposts
2636 Elm Hill Pike, Suite 120
Nashville, Tennessee 37214

Guideposts, *Ideals* and *Tales from Grace Chapel Inn* are registered trademarks
of Guideposts.

The characters and events in this book are fictional, and any resemblance to
actual persons or events is coincidental.

All Scripture quotations, unless otherwise noted, are taken from *The Holy Bible,
New International Version.* Copyright © 1973, 1978, 1984 International Bible
Society. Used by permission of Zondervan Bible Publishers.

Scripture quotations marked (KJV) are taken from *The King James Version of the
Bible.*

Library of Congress Cataloging-in-Publication Data has been applied for.

Cover by Deborah Chabrian
Design by Marisa Jackson
Typeset by Nancy Tardi

Printed and bound in the United States of America

10 9 8 7 6 5 4 3 2 1

GRACE CHAPEL INN

A place where one can be
refreshed and encouraged,
a place of hope and healing,
a place where God is at home.

Introduction

*I*t's starting to snow, and there are some wicked-looking dark clouds heading toward us from the west," Jane Howard said to her sisters as she came into the parlor of Grace Chapel Inn.

"A blizzard?" Louise Howard Smith, her oldest sister, looked up from her knitting. Her gaze went to the window. "In March?"

"Looks that way." A few crystalline flakes made Jane's long dark ponytail sparkle as she produced the small bundle of envelopes she had retrieved from the mailbox. "Did either of you listen to the latest weather report?"

"I heard the news at noon," Alice Howard said as she brought her younger sister a steaming cup of hot cocoa. "There was a large storm moving across the Appalachians toward us."

"I think it's here."

Concern appeared in Alice's gentle brown eyes. "The forecaster predicted ten to twelve inches of snow for central Pennsylvania northeast into eastern New England." She grimaced. "I was hoping it would skip us."

"Well, it didn't." Jane shivered as she gratefully exchanged the mail for the mug and cradled it between her chilled hands. "I wish spring would hurry up and get here. I'm so tired of cold and snow and more snow. I think my chilblains are getting frostbite."

"The next time you decide to go out to the mailbox, put on your coat and gloves first." Louise completed another row of stitches in the pullover she was making before she glanced at the darkening window. The scrolls of frost on the glass were almost the same shade of silvery white as her elegantly cropped hair. "I thought it felt a little colder than yesterday."

"I haven't felt anything since December," Jane complained as she picked up a crocheted throw and wrapped it around herself. "To think, for *this* I left sunny California."

"Sunny?" Alice snorted. "You used to complain all the time about how cold and damp it was in San Francisco when you lived there."

"True." Jane gave a theatrical shudder. "Maybe I should try moving to Florida. Or Brazil. Or the Sahara."

"A hot bath is what you need," Louise advised. "We should check the firewood in the event that we lose power again. May I see the mail, dear? I'm expecting a letter from Cynthia."

"Of course." Alice handed Louise the bundle before she returned to her chair and picked up the nursing journal she had been reading. "We don't have any guests scheduled to arrive, do we?"

"We don't have any reservations until next week. That's a blessing: With this storm the driving conditions will probably be atrocious." Louise put on the reading glasses that hung from a chain around her neck and sorted through the bundle. "Why, look at this." She extracted one thick envelope. "It's a letter from Mr. Venson."

"Ted wrote to us?" Jane came over to sit beside her on the sofa as Louise opened the envelope, which contained a single sheet of notepaper wrapped around a thick stack of glossy photographs. "Hey, he sent pictures too."

"He said that he would," Alice said. "I thought he had forgotten."

"'Dear Ladies,'" Louise read out loud from the letter, "'I am keeping my promise to send you copies of the photographs I took during our visit to Acorn Hill. I think that they tell the story of what happened to us far better than I ever could.'"

Jane chuckled. "People won't believe that story unless they *see* some pictures."

"I also have a surprise for you, but that I must inform

you of in April,'" her older sister continued to read. "'Who would have thought that what promised to be the most dismal holiday of my life would have turned out the way it did? Until April, Yours sincerely, Ted Venson.'"

"What a lovely note." Alice set aside her magazine as Louise passed the first of the photographs from the stack to her.

The snapshot showed six people, one of them a middle-aged man in a driver's cap, standing next to a small tour bus.

"Oh, I think I actually took this one. Ted handed me his camera and asked me to take a picture the day they arrived in town." Alice looked up. "Remember, Louise?"

"I doubt that I could forget, even if I tried," Louise said as she passed another photo of the group for Jane to see. "What an impossible situation that was."

Dimples appeared in Alice's cheeks. "Now you sound like you're quoting Max Ziglar."

"Max certainly looked depressed in this one." Jane handed her the second photo, then took another from Louise. "Yikes, and in this one too. Look at how he's chewing on that cigar."

The corner of Louise's mouth curled. "I rather thought that look—and those cigars—were permanent fixtures on Max Ziglar's countenance."

"Here's one of the group standing by a fireplace with

Viola Reed." Alice frowned. "Was Viola unwell that day? She seems a little pink in the face."

Louise shook her head. "Ted took that photo just after Laura Lattimer and Viola had a clash over Viola's English chandelier."

Jane perked up. "You mean those two got into a tussle and you never told us?"

"It was a verbal disagreement, dear, not a fistfight," Louise corrected. A self-deprecating smile brightened her face. "At the time I remember feeling very relieved that the group would only be in town for the Christmas home tour."

"This only proves that you'll never be a psychic, Louise." Jane picked up a snow globe from the side table and shook it. White snowflakes swirled around the three carolers inside. Across the room the wind moaned within the parlor's fireplace chimney. Her gaze grew thoughtful. "I wonder what we would have done and what choices we would have made, if only we'd known."

"Had I known, I think I might have gone to visit Cynthia for the holidays," Louise said wryly. "A daughter at Christmastime is a wonderful companion."

"Father used to say that everything happens for a reason." The next photograph made Alice laugh. "Why, Ted took a picture of the three of us that day too. He never mentioned it."

Jane chuckled. "Ted was sneaky."

Alice smiled at a photo of herself with Louise and Jane as they stood looking at one of the shop windows in town. There was snow in her younger sister's dark hair and on the shoulders of Louise's dark green jacket. They had all been carrying shopping bags filled with holiday purchases. "You know, all I could think about that morning was how wonderful it was going to be, spending a quiet Christmas at home with my sisters. . . ."

Chapter One

*W*inter had come to the little town of Acorn Hill, Pennsylvania, and brought with it crisp cold air, bright blue skies and just enough snow to adorn every rooftop with a shimmering cover of pure white.

Although the temperature had dropped enough since Thanksgiving to make hats, gloves and heavy coats a daily necessity, the residents of the small town welcomed the month of December with joy and expectation.

Christmas was only a week and a half away.

Signs of the season were everywhere, from the festive outdoor lighting and decorations that dressed up every home and business to the smiles and cheerful greetings shared by the busy residents. Every merchant had put up a grand holiday display, and passersby could view beautifully decorated Christmas trees through the windows of nearly every home.

This period just before Christmas was especially busy for the people residing in the little town. There were pres- ents to wrap, cookies to bake, relatives to meet and dinner menus to plan. Church committees held their end-of-the-year Christmas parties and no pastor in town was allowed to dine alone.

Enjoying the traditions of the holidays was something everyone looked forward to and indulged in, welcoming the time to express their faith, love for family, and thankfulness for the abundant blessings of life.

This year the three sisters who ran the bed and breakfast on the edge of town were particularly eager for Christmas to arrive. After busy months of looking after their many guests, Louise, Alice and Jane Howard felt they had earned some time for themselves, and had just closed Grace Chapel Inn through the weekend until after Christmas. They had looked forward to this time for so long and now they wanted nothing to interfere with their holiday enthusiasm.

"You know, it's lovely weather for a sleigh ride together with you," Alice sang as she brought the fresh evergreen branches in from the garden.

"We can't go riding, we have no sleigh," Jane said as she took a tray of tiny round cream-colored wafers from the oven. A rich, buttery scent filled the air as she set the cookies to cool on a rack.

Alice put the branches in the sink. "Okay, how about a snowball fight?"

"Tempting, and I would probably win, but no time for that either." Jane put her hands on her hips and surveyed the cooling racks. "I must bake. After I bake, I must wrap."

"Aren't you the ambitious one lately?"

"It's what I get for loving good food and my two wonderful sisters." She pretended to think for a moment. "No, I must shop first, *then* I must wrap."

"Goodness, don't be all work and no play," Alice teased as she brushed some snow clinging to the branches into the sink. "You don't want to end up being a dull girl, too, do you?"

"I'll be lazy and interesting after New Year's. Hey, you." Jane scooped up Wendell, the family tabby cat, as he jumped up onto the counter. "Now I know the smell of the cream is making you crazy, but these are really too rich for kitties. They'll give you an upset stomach."

Wendell meowed plaintively and butted his striped head into her chin, as if trying to convince her that he was more than up to the challenge.

"Trust me, I have something better." Jane retrieved a small can of shrimp-flavored feline treats from the cupboard and shook out a few on the floor. Wendell made a magnificent leap from her arms and fell on the treats, which he immediately started to devour.

"Have I earned a treat?" Alice asked as she leaned over

to peer into a small mixing bowl of green-tinted filling and then inspected the quarter-sized cookies. "Oh, how pretty. What are these, exactly?"

"I haven't thought up a name for them yet." Jane picked up one of the wafers that had cooled, added a dollop of filling and sandwiched it with another before she offered it to Alice. "Try one. I need some suggestions."

A test nibble revealed that the cookies were actually rounds of thin, flaky pastry lightly dusted on the outside with granulated sugar. The creamy middle added the perfect touch of richness.

Alice closed her eyes to savor the taste of Jane's pastry creation. "*Mmm.*"

"No mummy sounds." Jane pretended to look severe. "Besides, you *mmm* about everything I make."

"That's because I always want *mmm*more." Alice reached for another and then took a moment to study it. "They taste scrumptious, and they're so pretty and delicate too. I've never seen Christmas cookies like these."

"Well, I just invented them." Jane regarded the fruit of her labors and tried out some names. "Delicate Divines. Divine Delicates. Double Delicate Divinities." She sighed. "No, that's not going to work. 'Divinity' has already been used for candy."

Alice laughed. "Whatever you decide to call them, I think *you're* divine for making them." She ate the second cookie and sighed. "You'd better hide them, though, or I won't be responsible for how many I gobble up. They're so light they'd tempt the angels."

"Angel light cookies, that's perfect." Jane took a pen and wrote the name down on her recipe notebook. "You're a genius."

"You don't have to twist my arm. I'll be your name tester, anytime." Alice looked over as the door to the kitchen swung open. "Louise, you should be trying out Jane's new cookies."

"I could smell them baking, but I was preoccupied with checking out the last of our guests." Louise examined the counters, which were filled with racks of the cooling rounds. "Very nice, Jane. The perfect size for afternoon tea."

"Flattery gets you a cookie." Jane fixed another angel-light cookie and presented it to her with a flourish.

"Thank you, dear." Louise turned to Alice. "Are you finished collecting your evergreens outside? If so, I would like to make an early start on our shopping expedition."

The demands of running an inn year-round meant that the Howard sisters rarely had the opportunity to spend a day out together. In fact, they had not had an entire week off for themselves since transforming their childhood home into a bed and breakfast after the death of their father, Daniel. It was one of the reasons they had decided to reserve the time of Christmas exclusively for themselves.

"I'm just going to put these boughs in water so that they'll stay fresh until tonight. They're easier to work with that way," Alice said, reaching into the cabinet under the sink for the bucket stored there. "Will someone remind me to pick up some floral wire from Wild Things while we're in town? I need it for the wreath I'm planning to make."

"I'll add it to my list." Louise glanced at the slim gold watch on her left wrist. "Fred Humbert said he would deliver our tree tomorrow afternoon, so we should also bring the decorations down from the attic today, if possible."

"I think that tree we picked out is gorgeous," Jane said as she began piling wafers into an airtight container. "I love Douglas firs. So, where are we going to set it up this year?"

"The one we chose is too tall for the study." Louise considered the question for a moment. "There is no place in the parlor for it, either, unless we have Fred move the piano to one side."

"If we move the piano, you won't be able to play carols on Christmas Eve," Jane said. "I love the tree and all, but we have to have your music, Louise."

Her youngest sister's compliment made her chuckle. "Flattery will get you all the Christmas carols your heart desires."

"Since we won't have any guests over the holiday, why don't we put it up in the reception area?" Alice suggested as she added water to the bucket. "I know I loved rushing downstairs on Christmas morning to see that Santa had delivered the tree."

"Me too." Jane chuckled. "Poor Father, he probably spent most of the night hauling it in from the shed and setting it up and decorating it, and still he always acted surprised to see it."

"I think he was amazed that it had not fallen down," Louise said, her voice dry. "No matter how hard he tried, Father never could get a tree to stand up straight."

Jane laughed. "Come to think of it, they always did list a little to the left or right."

"But he made the holidays special for us." Alice felt a little pang of sorrow as she always did when she thought of Daniel Howard. "This Christmas I want to read Luke's version of the birth of Jesus out loud, the same way he did after he tucked us in. I'd like to make some homemade bird feeders too. Father always liked to hang those to decorate the trees out front, and the poor little birds can always use the seed."

"I have a bag of pinecones in the shed we can use." Jane took the last pan from the oven before she turned it off, then left the door open so that the heat would escape and help warm the kitchen. "Better add peanut butter and wild bird seed to the list, Louise."

"Good heavens, peanut butter and bird seed?" Aunt

Ethel said as she came into the kitchen. "What on earth are you mixing up now, Jane Howard?"

Daniel Howard's sister lived in the carriage house right next to Grace Chapel Inn, and popped in frequently to check on her nieces and share the latest gossip from town. Although she had strong opinions that were sometimes at odds with those of the sisters, Ethel Buckley regularly brought humor and happiness into their lives.

Today Ethel had dressed in a bright green, cable-knit sweater and matching slacks, and she sported a festive, pointed, green knit hat pulled over her short red hair.

"It's a classic recipe, Auntie Elf," Jane teased.

An enormous white pompom on the tip of Ethel's hat bobbed as she scanned her nieces' faces. "Please tell me you're not going to feed that muck to anyone."

"We sure are. You spread peanut butter over a pinecone and roll it in bird seed." Jane brought her fingers to her lips and kissed them. "It's delectable stuff."

"It is if you happen to have a beak and wings," Louise tacked on. "They're not for us, Aunt Ethel. They are bird feeders. We plan to hang them in our trees."

"Thank goodness." Ethel pressed a hand over her heart and then gave Jane a stern look. "I should make you give me the recipe for every single thing you feed me, anyway. Lord only knows what you put in that seafood gumbo you sent over last week."

"Well, there were those raw squid tentacles . . ." Jane laughed with delight at her aunt's wide eyes. "I'm kidding, I'm kidding."

"Keep it up, Miss Smarty." Ethel wagged her finger at her youngest niece. "You're going to get a lump of coal in your stocking." She regarded Alice and Louise. "So, how are you girls planning to spend your first day of vacation?"

"Today we're going to do some shopping," Alice told her. "We were so busy with guests last week that we never got to town."

Jane hung up her potholders. "Why don't you come with us? We'll spend money and show off your hat around town."

"I wish I could, dear, but I'm hosting a craft exchange at my house this morning. That's why I'm here. Do you still have those lacquer trays that you sent to Daniel from San Francisco?" She looked around the kitchen. "I need to borrow four of them."

"Sure." Jane retrieved the small black trays, which were hand painted with bamboo and varied Oriental flowers. "What's a craft exchange?"

"Some of the ladies from church get together and teach each other how to make a special holiday craft, like ornaments and such," their aunt said. "Florence Simpson usually hosts it, but she's gone until January. Carol Matthews is bringing her beads, which everyone loves, and the trays will keep them and the other small parts involved from rolling off the table."

Ethel was the director of Grace Chapel's church committees, and often volunteered to fill in as host for various meetings and study groups when their committee leaders were unavailable.

As their aunt tucked the trays into the tote bag she carried, she stopped and drew out something cylindrical wrapped in tissue paper.

"I almost forgot. I picked up a candle for your window while I was at a craft fair in Potterston. It's handmade and scented."

Alice unwrapped the candle, which was large, white, and beautifully decorated on the sides with holly leaves and berries made of red and green wax. The scent of peppermint from the candle mingled with the buttery fragrance of Jane's cookies. "It's lovely, Aunt Ethel."

"You have to put it in the front window on Christmas Eve," Ethel told them, "and keep it lit all night."

Louise frowned at that. "I would rather not leave a burning candle untended, Aunt."

"The woman at the craft show told me that it's a tradition for innkeepers," Ethel insisted. "She said that an inn owned by Christians keeps a candle burning in the window through Christmas Eve to light the way of the Holy Family, as well as to welcome guests. You girls know that you can't turn away any traveler who comes here on Christmas Eve either."

"I remember reading something about that," Alice said. "It comes from an old German custom. You burn the candle all night and welcome any visitor, in case the Christ Child might come by."

"We're closed for business until after Christmas," Jane reminded their aunt. "But we promise, on our honor as good Christian innkeepers, not to turn away any pregnant women being led around on donkeys."

"Don't make jokes about this, young lady," Ethel said, obviously not amused. "There are always good reasons for following the old ways."

The youngest Howard sister nodded gravely. "Like keeping all the Christmas candlemakers employed."

Ethel's stern mask cracked, and Alice laughed along with her aunt and sisters. She felt safe in the knowledge that no matter who came to the door on Christmas Eve, he would always find a warm welcome at Grace Chapel Inn.

Shopping in town was fun for the Howard sisters; it was a rare occasion that the three of them could do it together. They first went to the General Store to pick up some household items and found a jolly Santa collecting goods for the store's annual community Christmas food baskets drive. For the sisters' contribution to the cause, Santa gave them each a candy-cane pin made of twisted red-and-white chenille strips to wear on their coats.

"Bless you, ladies," said the jolly old elf, who was really the store manager in costume. "Santa couldn't ask for better helpers."

"Santa could put more chestnuts out in the produce section, though," Jane said and winked.

The sisters took a leisurely stroll down Berry Lane, stopping now and then to look in windows or step inside to make a purchase in one of the shops.

Louise was particularly drawn to the sterling silver service and serving cart displayed in the front window of Time for Tea. Wilhelm Wood, the owner, had displayed ceramic versions of the many cakes and treats of a genuine English high tea, and had so many different varieties of boxed and tinned tea stacked on the cart that she sighed with delight. "Silver is so heavy and impractical," she told her sisters, "but there is nothing quite as elegant."

"Look at that crystal honey server." Jane peered in. "What does he have in there, gold dust?"

"That or some very glittery honey," Alice said with a laugh.

Wilhelm noticed them and stepped outside to exchange greetings. "Are you contemplating a new tea service for the inn, ladies?"

"We are being sorely tempted by that and your teas, Wilhelm," Louise told him. "But the silver is a bit out of our price range."

"Wait right here." The shop owner disappeared inside, and returned with a small brown bag, which he handed to the eldest Howard sister. "These are some samples of my new holiday blends. Try them, let me know what you like and I'll make up a box of them for you. Christmas discount included."

They thanked Wilhelm and then walked on to the florist shop.

It was good to be out in the crisp, cold air, Alice thought. The combination of bright decorations and Christmas music and happy faces was positively exhilarating.

"That's the last item on our list," Louise said as they emerged from Wild Things. "Do you need anything else for your wreath, Alice?"

"No, I'm going to use some of the old ball ornaments we have from last year, and I already have a spool of metallic ribbon for the bow." Her stomach rumbled. "Is anyone else hungry?"

"I'm always hungry," Jane said. "Let's take these bags back to the car and stow them in the trunk. Then we won't have to bother with them at lunch."

As they walked to the parking lot behind Town Hall, the sisters exchanged greetings with friends and neighbors they passed who, like them, were out doing their holiday shopping. There were many visitors in town too, so the sidewalks were somewhat crowded, and occasionally the sisters had to stop and step aside to allow someone struggling with bundles to pass.

"I don't recall seeing this many people last December," Alice said as they made way for a young couple who emerged from the antique shop burdened with a large porcelain lamp and a tapestry-upholstered footstool. "Tourism seems to have picked up quite a bit."

"I have had to refer a number of last-minute requests for reservations to the Burgeron Inn in Potterston," Louise said. "The last time I called, the reception clerk told me that they were booked through to New Year's Day. All the other hotels and motels are filling up fast too."

Alice frowned. "Why are they so packed?"

"There's a parade and two conventions in Potterston, according to the *Innkeeper's Journal*," Jane said, referring to the trade magazine to which she subscribed. "The hotels will probably stay that way through Christmas." She gave Louise a mischievous look. "Sure you don't want to open our doors? We could probably fill all the guest rooms without any trouble."

"I've waited all year for this vacation, Jane." She gave her a stern look. "We're going to enjoy it, even if I must nail the front door closed."

A young man with black-rimmed glasses stepped up to the sisters. "Excuse me, ladies, but would one of you mind taking a photo of us?" He had a large, expensive-looking camera on a strap around his neck. "I've already adjusted it. All you have to do is frame and shoot."

"Sure, I'll try." Alice gingerly took the complicated-looking camera and peered through the frame window.

The young man was standing with two ladies and two other men by a minivan with a round logo on the door depicting a house and the words "Country Home Tours" scrolled around it. A middle-aged man wearing a driver's hat tried to step out of the picture, but one of the women urged him to remain in the shot. A couple of sour expressions suggested that not all were enthusiastic about the picture taking.

"Smile, everyone." Alice snapped the photo and then carefully handed the camera back to the visitor.

"I really appreciate it, ma'am," the young man said. "Happy holidays to you."

"Thanks." She grinned back. "The same to you and your friends."

Once they had secured their purchases in the car's trunk and had walked over to the Coffee Shop, Alice checked her watch.

"We'll still have some free time after lunch," she said, catching Louise's eye as she opened the door to the restaurant. "Would you like to do some browsing?"

Louise understood what she meant immediately. Both she and Alice had yet to find a gift for Jane. In years past she and her late husband, Eliot Smith, had sent her youngest sister a gourmet food basket, and Alice had sent her gift certificates, but now that Jane was living with them, they wanted to get her something more personal. They had discussed buying something for the kitchen or the gardens, but overseeing those areas was Jane's work.

"We should get her something for fun," Alice had said. "You know, something that she doesn't need or that she wouldn't buy herself."

The only problem was that Jane would not give them a clue regarding what she wanted.

Louise had even asked her sister point-blank what she would like for Christmas, but Jane had only shrugged and replied that anything would do. Alice's suggestion of browsing was clever; while they were walking through the stores they could pay more attention to Jane, who might show interest in something.

"That's fine," Jane said, evidently unaware she was the reason for it. "I love to browse."

"Good afternoon, ladies." June Carter, the owner of the Coffee Shop, came from behind the counter to greet them. A robust woman, she had the easy personality of someone who enjoyed being around other people. "Would you like a booth or a table?"

The middle-aged driver who had been with the group Alice had photographed excused himself as he passed by the sisters and went to use the pay phone outside.

"A booth," Louise said. An unfamiliar odor drifted near her face and made her nose wrinkle. "Is that cigar smoke I smell?"

"I do believe it is." June scanned the room. "Excuse me for one second, ladies." She strode to a table of five people, where she tapped a heavyset man on the shoulder. "Sir, I'm sorry, but there is no smoking permitted in the restaurant."

The man scowled up at her. "Why not?"

June blinked. "Out of courtesy for others." Because she had no ashtrays, she took an empty saucer from a nearby table and placed it in front of him. "I must ask you to put it out or smoke outside."

"You should have a sign up somewhere," the older man grumbled as he stubbed out the end of the big cigar he had just lit. "Can we order now or what?"

"Thank you for cooperating. I'll be with you in just a moment." June returned to the sisters and rolled her eyes as she picked up three menus. "Tourists."

Chapter Two

*J*une showed the sisters to the only unoccupied booth, and excused herself again. "Hope will be with you in just a minute." She went back to take the orders from the cigar smoker and his four companions, who were sitting a table away from the Howards.

"So where shall we browse first after lunch?" Louise asked as she opened her menu.

"I haven't been to the antique shop in a while," Alice said. "Or Sylvia's Buttons."

"I'd like to go to Fred's Hardware," Jane said, and then saw her sisters' expressions. "We need a new outdoor bulb for the porch light. The old one was flickering when I switched it off this morning."

"I suppose Fred's new train display has something to do with why you didn't pick up one at the general store earlier," Louise said.

"Not at all." Jane put on an innocent look. "If I had, I'd still have thought of some other sort of hardware we needed to give me the excuse."

"Let's not forget that we have gift baskets to make up for our friends, and tomorrow I would like to start delivering them," Louise said. "Perhaps we could go by Viola Reed's in the evening, after she closes the shop." Viola, who owned the Nine Lives Bookstore, was one of Louise's good friends.

"I promised Rose Bellwood that we would come by to see the Nativity presentation at her farm," Alice said. "She mentioned that Samuel has built a new crèche for this year's performance."

"I'm not interested in getting my money back," a low, gloomy voice said.

Jane and her sisters could not help looking at the speaker at the table across from them. It was the man who had been smoking and he was evidently discussing something with his four companions.

"Those are the people I took the picture of, aren't they?" Alice murmured.

Jane recognized the young man in the black-rimmed glasses from the street. At first glance the two women and the older man seemed like nice, contented people, but the big cigar smoker looked as unhappy as he sounded.

"Their problems are their problems," the man continued, jabbing the air with his unlit cigar. "They have an obligation to us and we can't let them walk all over us like this."

Jane thought he looked like the type of man who

expected people to jump when he snapped his fingers, but there was something else about him. She sensed a deep melancholy from the tone of his voice and the brooding quality of his dark eyes. Had it been any other time of year, she might not have noticed. But now, during the holidays, when everyone else seemed so happy, the big man's dismal expression made him stand out from his companions.

"I didn't see anything about refunds or rescheduling, but let me check the brochure again," a thin, suddenly agitated-looking woman with spiky short brown hair and rather heavy makeup said. Her big, dangling silver earrings bobbed as she sorted through her purse. "We could call the Better Business Bureau and lodge a complaint."

"I don't want to make complaints." The cigar smoker twisted in his seat, making the large platinum and diamond clip he wore on his tie flash. "We purchased the full package, not two-thirds of it. I don't think we should leave until we get what we paid for."

Jane wondered what could have been bought that someone would only deliver in thirds.

"Be reasonable, Max," the other woman in the group said. Salt-and-pepper curly hair framed her plump face, which was as pleasant and calm as her voice. "What happened is no one's fault. Naturally the company can't send a replacement. People want to be home with their families during the holidays."

Now Alice looked up from her menu and started watching the other table.

"They should have thought of that before they scheduled these dates." Max clamped his cigar in his teeth and chomped on the end. "This is no way to run a business. Doesn't matter that it's Christmastime. If it were my company, I'd have had at least two replacements on standby, ready to get to work."

Jane's sympathy quickly faded. "I bet one of them would be named *Cratchit*," she said under her breath.

Louise gave her a direct look. "It's not polite to eavesdrop on other people's conversations, dear."

"This isn't eavesdropping." Jane gestured to the short distance between tables. "This is being made to overhear."

Alice leaned close. "Should we ask June to move us to another spot?"

Louise shook her head and gave the other group a slightly disdainful glance. "I'm sure they'll quiet down when their meal is served. Just ignore them."

But trying not to listen in on the conversation at the other table was difficult for Jane. Especially when what they were discussing sounded so interesting.

"Do we really need a replacement?" the young man with the camera asked. "After all, we are expected. We'll just explain what happened and ask the people to let us go through by ourselves."

"I don't know about that, Ted." The fifth member of the group, a lean, tanned man with thick white hair, finished his coffee and patted his trim mustache with a napkin. "The residents might object to us simply wandering around unsupervised. These are private homes, after all."

What on earth are they talking about? Jane decided she was not leaving the restaurant until she found out.

The pleasant-looking older woman excused herself from the table.

The thin woman with the silver earrings made a rude sound. "We can be trusted to go about on our own. Are we schoolchildren, Allan?"

At that moment the other woman from the group was passing by the Howards' table on her way to the restroom, and Jane heard her murmur, "If the shoe fits."

~

Really, people should have better manners when they are in a restaurant, Louise thought. *The next thing you know one of them will take out a cellular phone.*

Hope Collins, their waitress, provided a welcome distraction by coming to the table to take their orders. "Hello, ladies. What can I get for you today?"

Alice asked for a tuna sandwich and clam chowder. As the waitress wrote on her order pad, Alice added, "Hope, do you know those people over there?"

Hope glanced over her shoulder and then lowered her voice. "They're tourists staying over at a hotel in Potterston. One of the ladies in the group—that nice, older one—told me that they've been going around seeing historic Pennsylvania homes for the last ten days. Sounds like some sort of new Christmas vacation package thing that's just been started this year."

"Is something troubling them?" Jane asked Hope.

Louise set down her menu. "Now, Jane . . ."

"I'm just asking." She handed her menu to the waitress. "From the sound of things, they're having some kind of difficulty."

"Well, from what I've heard, their tour guide slipped on a patch of ice just after they got to town yesterday," the waitress said. "They had to take him over to the hospital. They came back today, expecting a new guide, but no one showed up. I don't think the company running the tour has anyone to fill in."

"I remember that gentleman coming up on my ward last night," Alice said. "He's going to be fine, but his ankle was fractured in two places. The doctor had to put him in a heavy leg cast, so he won't be able to walk on it for some time."

"How terrible!" Louise felt a pang of guilt over her earlier thoughts. Of course, the group had the right to be upset. She just wished they would discuss their problem somewhere else, away from her highly sympathetic and susceptible sisters.

Jane gave her order for a bowl of chili with a side salad, and then asked, "Do you know whose homes they were scheduled to tour, Hope?"

"June said that the Bellwoods' and Miss Reed's were two of them." The waitress turned to Louise. "What can I get for you, Mrs. Smith?"

After she placed her order, Louise tried to block out the continued grumbling coming from the tourists' table by discussing holiday plans with her sisters. This year she had her heart set on getting out to visit more of their friends, and on participating in some of the community gatherings and celebrations.

Despite her efforts, however, both Jane's and Alice's attention—particularly Jane's—kept drifting over to the five unhappy faces around the other table.

"I know what you two are thinking," Louise said after they had finished lunch. "Have you forgotten that we promised ourselves this vacation? And how hard we have worked to arrange it?"

"I know, Louise. It's just . . ." Alice searched for the right words.

"It's Christmas," Jane answered for her, "and we should do something."

Louise sighed. She loved her sisters dearly, but sometimes

they exasperated her to no end. "What can we possibly do for these people?"

"Well, one of us could fill in for their guide," Jane said.

"It wouldn't take much time to show them around," Alice said, very tentatively. "Perhaps an hour here and there at the most." When Louise did not reply, she added, "We could take turns."

Her silver eyebrows rose. "You are assuming that you already have my participation."

"Oh, come on, Louise. We were planning to visit our friends anyway, weren't we?" Jane flipped her ponytail over her shoulder as she sat back. "If we take them around, it'll just be like visiting. Only we'll be bringing some extra people with us."

"I fear it may not be that simple." Louise placed her napkin next to her plate. "The group is obviously expecting a professionally guided tour, something none of us is really qualified to provide."

"Well, we could tell them up front that we're simply good Samaritans and not professional tour guides." Her youngest sister put her hand over hers. "Please, Louise. 'Tis the season, let's help make these poor folks feel jolly."

Louise cast another doubtful glance at the group. Some of them did not look very pleasant, particularly the biggest man.

"It would be the Christian thing to do," Alice added gently.

Louise did not consider herself a selfish woman, and

she did believe in being a good Christian and helping people whenever she could.

Just not this week.

Yet there was no way she could look at her sisters'
hopeful faces, or the dejected ones at the other table, and
not feel selfish.

"Oh, very well. We can offer to help." When Alice and
Jane started to talk at the same time, Louise held up one
hand. "I only want you both to remember something: Taking
a group of strangers around to see other people's homes
was not my idea of how we should spend our vacation."

"Don't be such a worrywart," Jane chided. "It'll be fun.
You'll see."

⤳

Since Jane had been the one to propose the idea, she volunteered to be the one to approach the group about their
dilemma. She was also more outgoing with strangers than
Alice was and more at ease with them than was Louise.

"We didn't mean to eavesdrop," Jane said after she had
walked over and exchanged greetings with the group, "but
my sisters and I couldn't help overhearing your discussion.
If you'd like, we'd be happy to take you around on the home
tour."

"That's a very kind offer," Allan Hansford said as his
white mustache framed his smile. He had introduced himself as a retired architect, and like her older sister he had

very keen, light blue eyes. "But we don't want to put anyone to any trouble."

"It's better than sitting around the hotel doing nothing," Max Ziglar said. His strong features were filled with as much dreariness as his deep voice. "There's nothing in it for you, though."

Jane frowned. "We're not expecting anything, sir."

"What Max is trying to say is that if you're thinking of charging us for the pleasure, you can forget it," said Laura Lattimer as she reapplied lipstick that matched her fingernails, handbag and bright red designer outfit perfectly. She had said she was an interior decorator. "I've already spent too much money on this trip."

"Max, Laura, please," Edwina Welles said, her tone as gently reproving as only an experienced grammar-school teacher's could be. She gave Jane an apologetic look. "We're all a little tired, I'm afraid. We've spent so much time cooped up in the van, and now to face the return trip without so much as a break..." she moved her shoulders. "I have to admit, I'm not looking forward to it either. Still, there's not much we can do, under the circumstances."

"I'm not going to sit in a hotel," Max insisted, tapping one finger against the tabletop. "Either the company provides a replacement or I'm staying here for at least the day."

"I guess even a walk around town beats staring at four hotel room walls," Ted admitted.

"You'll just end up spending more money," Laura predicted. "If this lady doesn't get any out of you."

"I understand how you feel." Jane was starting to wonder, though, if Max Ziglar ever smiled or if Laura Lattimer even understood the definition of Christian charity. "Please be assured that my sisters and I don't want to charge you anything. We're going to be visiting the homes on your tour anyway: The people who own them are our friends. We only wanted to offer our help." She met Max's dark gaze. "Absolutely free of charge."

"Well, I'm all for it." Ted Venson checked the snap on the case of his camera before hanging it around his neck. He pushed his thick-lensed glasses higher on the bridge of his prominent nose before he added, "I need to take at least three more rolls of film to round out my portfolio and these homes are rumored to be the best on the tour. I'm really looking forward to shooting them."

"Are you a professional photographer, Mr. Venson?" Jane asked.

"Not exactly," he admitted. "I work in the camera section of a department store and I take portrait photographs. You know, cute babies, families and so on. But I do my own photography on the side, and I'd like to go freelance and start selling my own work to magazines and publishers."

"Freelancing." Max's voice went heavy with disapproval. "You can't support a wife and family when you don't have a steady paycheck coming in, boy. You'd do better to forget this artistic nonsense and hold on to that job of yours."

"Oh, I am." Ted touched the gold wedding band on his left hand and a pained expression came over his face. "This is one last shot at my dream. If I can't sell these photos, I'll stick to family portraits."

Jane felt sympathy for the young man. When she had left home, she had pursued her own dreams with a single-minded intensity. But she knew that not everyone could have that opportunity.

"If you're certain this won't put out you or your sisters, then I'd be delighted to have you as our guides," Allan said.

"So would I." Edwina leaned to the side and smiled over at Louise and Alice, who were watching them.

The big businessman subjected Jane to another long, silent stare. Obviously he was reluctant to trust her, Jane thought, but why? *What makes you so suspicious of people, Max Ziglar?*

"Max, it would seem that we've been outvoted." Laura put her lipstick away and gave Jane a decidedly narrow look. "I do hope this is not going to be a complete waste of my time. That is one thing I absolutely cannot abide. My time is precious and, truth be told, I'd rather spend it back in the city."

For a moment the interior decorator reminded Jane of Florence Simpson, one of the more difficult women at church. Florence was the type who would not only look a gift horse in the mouth, but would hold off accepting it until she had weighed, measured and X-rayed it. And only then if it came with an appraisal.

"We'll do our best, Miss Lattimer. Let me bring my sisters over now so you can meet them." Laura's haughty remark made her repeat what she had told her sisters. "I think this will be a terrific experience for all of us."

⌒

"I think this will be a complete disaster for all of you," was the prediction Ethel Buckley made that evening over dinner at the inn.

Alice looked over at Louise, who seemed to be in silent agreement, and at Jane, who had a decidedly militant gleam in her eyes. "We haven't even started yet, Aunt Ethel."

"If you had the sense the good Lord gave a rabbit, Alice Howard, you'd call the whole thing off."

"Stop being so optimistic, Auntie," Jane said. "All this enthusiasm and confidence will make our expectations skyrocket."

Her aunt glared. "What were you girls thinking, agreeing to take on this tour group? You don't know anything about these people and you're certainly not responsible for them. They hired a company to bring them here for a tour. Why aren't *they* doing something about it? What sort of tour is this?"

"From what I understand, this is the first time the tour

company has scheduled a Christmas homes tour to visit Acorn Hill. This group is being used as a test for the town, to decide if they want to bring their groups here on a regular route." Louise unfolded her napkin and placed it in her lap. "The tour begins in Philadelphia and makes several visits to different towns over a period of ten days. The group pays a reasonable package price, which includes hotel accommodations and transportation."

"How did they decide on what houses to visit here in Acorn Hill?" Ethel asked.

"The company ran an ad in the *Acorn Nutshell*, inviting locals to make their homes available for the tour," Alice said. "In exchange, the company will make a donation in the host's name to Toys for Tots."

"It's a nice idea and could turn out to be good for the inn," Jane said. "If the tour company is looking for an annual package deal for accommodations, we might be able to offer them a discounted rate and have their groups stay here."

"If they are small groups," Louise added.

"Business is one thing, but I still don't see how not having a guide for these people has suddenly become your responsibility," their aunt insisted.

"It's Christmas, Aunt," Alice reminded her as she passed around the cloth-covered basket of hot rolls. "They're visitors to our town, they've had some bad luck and now we're simply trying to help out the poor souls."

"Poor souls, my Aunt Frances." Ethel snorted. "June told me that Ziglar fellow wears a fancy tie clip with a diamond the size of a golf ball. She also said that he paid for his lunch from a roll of bills that was three inches thick."

"June should have her eyes checked. The diamond was barely a full carat." Louise steepled her fingers. "What, pray tell, has Max Ziglar's wealth to do with whether or not we show them around, Aunt?"

"Only that it's obvious he could buy and sell this town, and yet he's accepting charity from you girls. And I'm not even sure he deserves it." Ethel took a roll and passed the basket to Jane. "No rich man can be a good Christian. Jesus told that to a wealthy young man in Mark, chapter ten, verse twenty-three."

"Jesus said it was hard for the rich to enter the kingdom of God," Alice corrected. "I taught a Bible study lesson about wealth and Christianity to my ANGELs before Thanksgiving."

"That sounds about right to me," Jane said.

"You're really determined to do this." Ethel put down her roll and looked around the table. "None of you have ever given a homes tour before, have you? How are you going to do it? When do you start?"

"We're going to discuss that now," Alice said.

"Let me get the brochure Mrs. Welles gave me." Jane rose and retrieved her purse from the counter, then brought the pamphlet back to the table. "There are four houses on the tour," she said, reading from the back. "Those of Viola Reed, Joseph and Rachel Holzmann, Mayor Lloyd Tynan, and Samuel and Rose Bellwood." She handed the tour literature to Louise. "We should be able to do all of them in three days, don't you think?"

"Three days? Is that enough time to visit three houses and a farm?" Ethel frowned, then inched her chair closer to Louise's so that she could read over her niece's shoulder.

"I believe that if the weather holds, we should be able to complete the entire tour in three days with little difficulty," Louise said.

"Good." Alice had been worried about the time schedule.

"This says four days in the beautiful town of Acorn Hill," Ethel read from the brochure.

"The tour here was originally planned for four days plus extra time in the area for shopping and resting up," Jane clarified, "but the group lost a day because their guide was injured and they have to return to the city on Saturday. That's why we agreed to start tomorrow."

"We should each take the group for one day," Louise said. "Alice, since you have to prepare to take your ANGELs out caroling tomorrow, I'll accompany the group to Viola's in the morning, and the Holzmanns' in the afternoon. You can take them to Mayor Tynan's on Thursday morning, and Jane can escort them to the Bellwoods' on

Friday evening while you and I go to the children's ward party at the hospital."

"That seems reasonable to me." The phone at the reception desk rang, and as Jane was already up, she left the kitchen to answer it.

"Doing this will cut your vacation in half," Ethel persisted.

"Not precisely," Louise said.

"This was Jane's idea, wasn't it?" Their aunt glanced at the door. "I thought you closed the inn for the holidays so that you could have this time together as a family. Now you're letting Jane waste it looking after a bunch of people who aren't even staying at your inn."

"We'll still have plenty of time for our vacation, Aunt Ethel," Alice assured her. "It's only for three days and then they'll be on their way home."

"I don't know, Alice." Her aunt shook her head slowly. "I have a very bad feeling about this."

"Alice, it's a Mr. Baldwin for you," Jane said as she came back into the kitchen. Her aunt was still looking rather peevish, so she retrieved the small jelly roll cake she had made for dessert and brought it to the table. "Here, Auntie. Have some cake. It's low fat."

Ethel sighed. "You always say that, but my hips always look bigger in the morning. I'll have to walk to town tomorrow to work off the calories." Her aunt gave into temptation and helped herself to a thin slice. "Oh, by the way, Jane, you haven't said a word about what you'd like to have for Christmas yet."

Your unconditional support for anything I decide to do for the next calendar year, thought Jane. "Anything would be just fine," she said.

"Anything is not specific enough." Ethel waved her fork for emphasis. "Anything could be *anything*, from a black velvet painting of *The Last Supper* to a red and yellow beanie hat with a propeller attached to the crown."

"I'm allergic to black velvet," Louise said at once.

Jane turned around from the stove and feigned surprise. "Really? Since when?"

"Since people stopped wearing it and started painting portraits of the Lord and Elvis Presley on it." Louise winced as she regarded their aunt. "Nothing with a propeller attached, Aunt Ethel. I beg you."

"You see?" Ethel spread her hands and put on her best martyred look as she turned back to Jane. "You have to give me a better idea before I get into trouble with your sister."

It didn't help that what Jane wanted for Christmas was one thing she could never have.

"I have everything I could possibly want," she said at last. "A little something for the kitchen or garden will do fine."

Alice returned in time to overhear the latter, and gave Louise an odd look before she sat down. "That was Mr. Baldwin from the tour company. He wanted to express his appreciation for our taking charge of the group. He's going to e-mail the tour literature to us and has offered to pay us the standard rate one of his guides would receive."

"The literature will be very helpful," Louise said, "but it's not necessary to compensate us."

"Take the money, Louise," her aunt said. "By this time tomorrow, you'll probably feel like you've earned it."

Jane was a little surprised when her oldest sister shook her head. She knew Louise was only going along with the idea because she and Alice had cajoled her into it.

"This is the season of giving, especially to people in need," Louise said. "We'll take this opportunity to be Good Samaritans."

"All right." Ethel shook her head. "I only hope you don't end up needing some charity yourselves."

Chapter Three

*L*ouise left Grace Chapel Inn early the next morning to drive into town and meet the five visitors for the first part of the tour. A call from her daughter Cynthia the night before had helped lift her spirits and even made her laugh at herself.

"You're going to be a tour guide, Mother?" Her daughter had laughed. "I could see you showing people around a concert hall or an art museum, but country homes?"

"I am full of hidden depths that you don't know about, my dear," Louise had said firmly. "I only wish I could be spending the time with you."

"I'm sorry I couldn't make it there for the holidays, but you know how publishing is. Christmas is a madhouse for us." Cynthia had sighed. "I promise, next year I'm taking two weeks off."

Louise still felt somewhat resentful about the task of supervising the tour group, particularly on a day when she had planned to sleep in a little and do nothing more strenuous than hang some tree ornaments and tie ribbons around gift boxes.

The Bible does not say how much work it is to be a Good Samaritan, she thought as she turned off Chapel Road onto Hill Street. *Or how early one must get up to serve as one.*

Louise had arranged to meet the tour group and their driver in front of Town Hall, and she saw them as she drove into the back parking lot. The five visitors looked a little happier this morning, with the exception of Max Ziglar, who appeared as happy as a man being sent to his own execution. He was puffing on a large cigar and sending out white clouds of smoke all around him.

As Louise walked around the building to join the group, she tried to set her thoughts in order. *The Bible does not say anything about a grumpy Good Samaritan, either. I willingly agreed to do this. I will do my part cheerfully.* The pungent smell of Max's cigar reached her sensitive nose. *But those cigars will have to go.*

"Good morning, everyone." She took a moment to introduce herself to the driver, the pleasant middle-aged man they had seen the day before, and then she addressed the group. "As we discussed at the Coffee Shop, today we will be touring a Queen Anne Victorian house owned by Viola Reed, and a German Inglenook house owned by Joseph and Rachel Holzmann."

"How much do you know about historic architecture, Mrs. Smith?" Laura Lattimer asked.

This interior decorator had a catty way of speaking that made the most innocent question sound snide, Louise decided. It was fortunate that her years in the academic world had taught her how to deal with such passive-aggressive tactics.

"Please, call me Louise. I know more than the average person, I believe. My husband and I bought a nineteenth-century Greek revival home in Philadelphia when we were married. We spent many happy months researching the period so that we could correctly restore the original floors and interior woodwork."

Louise nearly smiled at the interior decorator's visible surprise, but the smell of Max's cigar commanded her immediate attention.

Now to deal with this once and for all. Louise did not like confronting people about their personal habits, but this one was too intrusive and unhealthy to ignore.

"Max, I would appreciate it if you would put that out and refrain from smoking anything for the remainder of the tour," she said, keeping her tone polite but firm.

"Why?"

"All of the homes we will be visiting belong to non-smokers. Also, cigar smoke has a pervasive odor that is very offensive to people who do not smoke." *Like me.* She met his gaze. "It will also be a kindness to your lungs and ours."

"You sound like my secretary," he grumbled, but obliged her by turning away to discard the cigar in a nearby ashstand.

When Max's back was turned, Edwina gave Louise a wide smile and silently mouthed the words *thank you so much*.

The group piled back into the van and the driver followed Louise as she drove her car to Viola Reed's home. Once the group had disembarked, the driver told her that he would return within the hour.

The five visitors were already examining the exterior of Viola's home with great interest.

"According to the literature your tour company provided for us, I am supposed to recite some facts about Queen Anne style homes, which are probably the most familiar examples of Victorian architecture," Louise said as she set down the basket she had brought from the car on the porch step. "But I would much rather tell you about Miss Reed's home in my own words."

"Please do, Louise," Allan Hansford said.

"My friend Viola Reed is a very well-read, practical woman and, shall we say, has very little patience with the realm of fantasy and nonsense. A house like this"—she lifted a hand to point out the ornate white gingerbread trim above the porch—"seemed to me far too fanciful to suit her down-to-earth nature."

"It doesn't look very practical," Laura murmured.

"The first time Viola invited me to her home, I thought I had arrived at the wrong house. In fact, I checked the address twice before I went up to knock on the door." Louise gazed up at the two-story turret, which had three long, oval-topped windows. "Even then, I almost expected someone else to answer it."

Everyone chuckled at that.

"It's rather like a little castle, isn't it?" Edwina commented. "You almost expect to see a princess standing in one of those upper windows and a prince wandering around down here calling, 'Rapunzel, Rapunzel!'"

"Very true, Edwina. As I visited a few more times, I began to see the warmth and grace in the design," Louise continued. "In a sense, houses are like people. There are some that have qualities that are not readily apparent on the surface. You have to get to know them before you can properly appreciate them."

"That's a lovely analogy," Allan said. "If I were still teaching design seminars, I'd steal it."

"I'm curious about something, Louise," Edwina said. "I've seen other Queen Anne houses and they are always painted in pastel and white colors, even if the surrounding houses are not. Why is that?"

"Light colors are traditional, as they best show the

uniqueness of the carved trims and other structural detailing," Allan said, and then gave Louise an apologetic look. "I'm sorry, I didn't mean to butt in."

"Please don't apologize," she told him. "I appreciate your expertise, especially since I couldn't have answered that question." Louise picked up her basket and escorted the group up the short, wide set of stairs onto the generous, open, wrap-around porch.

"Viola Reed also owns and operates the Nine Lives Bookstore in town." Louise stopped as a thought occurred to her and she turned toward the group. "Does anyone have an allergy to cats?" After receiving negative responses all around, she smiled. "I ask because Viola is very fond of them, as you will discover shortly." She went up and rang the doorbell.

Viola opened the door a moment later. A gentle waft of warm air scented with cinnamon and evergreen greeted the visitors.

"Good morning, Louise. I've been expecting you. Oh, you brought me a present." She gave her a brief hug as she accepted the sisters' gift basket of cookies and treats, and then nodded to the group. "Welcome to my home."

They filed into the front foyer, where Viola showed them the old-fashioned oak coat shelf with turned pegs from which they could hang their hats, scarves and coats. The bookshop owner was wearing a dull-gold, knit pant-suit with one of her trademark scarves, this one with a delightful pattern of old-fashioned Christmas ornaments embroidered in gold thread on white satin, with a tinsel-like, hand-knotted, metallic gold fringe.

"Smile, Louise," Ted said as he raised his camera to snap a shot of her beside Viola.

Louise held up her hand. "Please, Ted, I would rather you not take photos of me, if you don't mind. I am the *least* photogenic person I know, and even with your skill you would not enjoy the result."

Rather than being offended, he chuckled and nodded. "I understand. My wife claims that she would never have married me if she had seen a picture of me first."

"What a big foyer!" Laura said, looking toward the wide, oak staircase with its elegantly turned newels and solid balustrade. "You could park a bedroom or sitting room right in here."

"Yes, but why would you want to?" Ted said, earning a glare from the interior decorator.

"The large entry hall is a typical feature of a Queen Anne home," Allan said. "It's supposed to give a grand first impression and symbolize the owner's prosperity."

Laura seemed to like that answer, for she took out a handheld device and wrote something with a stylus on its small screen.

"It also comes in handy when you have six people visit at the same time." Viola bent to pick up one of her cats who had come to investigate, and scratched around the black-and-white spotted feline's neck. "Come into the parlor for a minute. I want to put this basket by the tree."

On the way there, Louise pointed out the swags made of living holly and ivy grown in Viola's garden, to which she had tied bundles of real cinnamon sticks with gilt ribbons to the greenery.

"That accounts for the lovely scent in the air," Edwina said. She paused to look up at the double-hooped swag hanging directly over the entrance to the parlor. "Oh my goodness. That's beautiful."

Made of evergreens entwined with spiky-leafed holly, this swag was much more lavishly decorated. Among the greenery were faux fruit, golden miniature ornaments, green satin ribbons and tiny electric candles. The lavish swag also supported a small cluster of dark-green leaves and waxy white berries hanging from the center.

"If I'm not mistaken, that's mistletoe, isn't it?" Edwina said. "I've never seen it displayed with such grandeur."

"You're admiring my Kissing Bough," Viola told her. "Hanging it over a doorway is a very old English custom that predates the Christmas tree."

"I assume anyone caught standing beneath it must still

pay the time-honored penalty?" Allan asked as he joined Edwina under the bough. When Viola nodded, the retired architect grinned. "I love old traditions."

He gave the schoolteacher a friendly kiss on the cheek and made her blush and laugh.

The way Max Ziglar quickly stepped around the mistletoe so as not to pass under it amused Louise. *Apparently not everyone loves old traditions.*

The average-sized room seemed much bigger, thanks to Viola's decor, which was classic French provincial in pale pink, blue and white tones. The furnishings were dainty without being fussy, and the eggshell-colored wallpaper with a tiny embossed fleur-de-lis pattern lent a delicate touch.

This was the sort of room in which one played Chopin, or Debussy, Louise had always thought. It was a shame that Viola did not have a piano.

The bookshop owner had carried over the dainty, year-round decor in her holiday decorations, which were all in shades of white, silver and gold, including those on the Christmas tree, which was crowned with a gold star. White satin ribbons chased with metallic gold and silver threads cascaded from the star and were woven around the simple, glass silver and gold balls and crocheted white snowflakes adorning the branches.

"I keep this parlor for company, as the windows provide a lovely view of the flower garden in the spring." Viola placed Louise's gift basket on a table by the bay windows. "You'll see the glass is the same throughout the house, with the large solid pane in the lower sash and the smaller panes in the upper."

"Are they the original windows, Miss Reed?" Allan asked.

"Some are. This one here is." She tucked the cat in one arm so she could point to one of the small glass squares. "The rippling effect is natural. Some say glass distorts from weather changes and heat. Others say it's due to flaws in the glass when it was made."

"It's not weather or heat, it's manufacturing flaws," Allan said. "Prior to the 1920s, plate glass was made by casting, rolling, and even handblowing cylinders that were cut and spread flat. Unfortunately, all these methods created inherent flaws in the glass, which rippled it and made variants in thickness."

Viola's eyebrows arched. "So all those stained glass windows with the rippled glass in them—"

"Were rippled when they were originally installed," Allan finished, giving her a grin. "As were your windows, Miss Reed."

Edwina went over to the fireplace mantel, where Viola had hung more than a dozen stockings knitted out of red, white and green wool. "What nice handiwork. How many little ones do you have, Miss Reed?"

"Fourteen at present, but I wouldn't call them all little ones." She placed the black-and-white cat on a tufted footstool. "Gatsby here, for example, weighs at least seventeen pounds."

Laura pressed a hand against her chest. "I thought you meant you had fourteen *children*."

"I do. Furry, four-legged children."

Max snorted. "Seems like a lot of fuss to make over some animals."

"Being kind to animals is a way to honor the season," Viola said, rather pointedly. "Remember that the lowly animals were the ones who shared their stable and provided a manger on the night Christ was born."

"I think it's a wonderful way to show affection for your pets," Edwina said firmly. "My husband and I have two dogs, and I'm going to make them stockings as soon as I get home."

"I'm glad to hear it. We can never do enough for our animal friends. Now, if you're all up to a little climbing, I'll show you the bedrooms and bath upstairs," Viola said.

On the way to the second floor, the group passed a large assortment of colorful masks adorning the length of the long wall by the stairs.

"Those look almost like carnival masks," Ted commented as he paused and lifted his camera to take several shots of the collection.

"Miss Reed's family immigrated to the United States from England, and like most Europeans, they brought their unique holiday traditions with them." Louise smiled at her friend. "However, as I'm not familiar with the custom, I'll have to impose on her to explain the customs behind the masks."

"Female frippery, most likely," Max muttered.

"Those are mummers' masks that are typical of costumes worn in England centuries ago," Viola said as she reached the second-floor landing. "Every year for the last one hundred years, the Mummers Parade has been held on New Year's Day in Philadelphia, where my family originally settled. These masks are part of the elaborate costumes worn by those who march in that festive event."

As they toured the bedrooms on the second floor, Viola mentioned other English holiday customs, such as hanging mistletoe, burning the Yule log and celebrating Boxing Day.

"Since the thirteenth century, the twenty-sixth of December has been a national holiday in England," Viola said as she led them into what had once been a child's nursery. When she refurnished it as a guest room, Viola had preserved the green and yellow color scheme, and had a small collection of children's books displayed in an ark-shaped shelving unit, lending a delightful air to the room. "The name 'Boxing Day' is believed to have originated from the churches' tradition of distributing the contents of their poor boxes on that day."

"Oh, I thought it meant the day you had to clean up all the gift boxes," Ted said after he had taken several photos. "Why do they celebrate it *after* Christmas instead of before, Miss Reed?"

"My father told me it might have been because servants were required to work on Christmas Day, but were allowed to spend the following day with their own families." Viola went over to the bookcase and absently straightened a few of the slim volumes. "The gentry were said to have boxed up their leftover food and presented it along with gifts to their servants before they left, which may also have contributed to the holiday's name."

"Boxing Day is also known as St. Stephen's Day," Louise said. "Stephen happens to be the first man in the Bible to be killed for following the teachings of Christ."

Edwina came over to admire the books. "I've noticed that you have bookcases in all the bedrooms. Is your personal library very large?"

"Probably more so than the average person's. I use the back parlor downstairs as my reading room, but I like to have books around me, wherever I am in the house." Viola removed a red, leather-bound volume with a knight in armor riding a horse from a castle and the title *Book Trails* embossed in Gothic lettering on the front cover. "My mother gave me this set when I was a girl. They were my first hardcover books."

"How many books do you think you've read in your lifetime, Miss Reed?" Ted asked.

"I don't know, I'm not dead yet," Viola said, then smiled at his expression. "What I mean to say is, I don't keep count, young man. I read a great deal, so I would imagine it is somewhere in the tens of thousands."

Gatsby, who had followed them upstairs, went over to a wooden toy chest and began pawing at the front panel. His plaintive meows made Viola chuckle.

"Someone wants one of his toys." She went over, opened the chest and took out a small, furry object.

Laura gasped. "Please tell me that's not a mouse."

"Never fear, it's just a toy." Viola turned a small key on the side of the mouse several times and then released it on the floor, where it began scurrying about just as a real mouse would.

Gatsby immediately tried to pounce on the scampering toy, leaping and swatting at it with his paws. Everyone chuckled at his antics, with the exception of Max, who stepped away from the excited feline.

Louise looked down as another of Viola's cats, a beautiful ivory Siamese with dark brown ears and muzzle, slipped into the room. It crept silently across the floor, its light blue eyes intent on the toy mouse. Max took another step backward just as it rushed forward and the Siamese barely avoided getting stepped on.

"Hey now!" The businessman grabbed the corner of a nearby dresser to keep his balance. "Where did that one come from?"

"Oh, Anna, come here." As Gatsby caught the toy mouse and rolled over onto his back as if wrestling it, Viola bent over and swept the Siamese up in her arms. "You always have to make a grand entrance, don't you, pretty girl?"

"Anna?" Edwina asked.

"I've named all my cats after characters from literary classics," the bookstore owner explained. "Anna is named for Margaret Landon's heroine in *Anna and the King of Siam*. Gatsby is rather obvious."

"You should keep these animals under control," Max said, his expression more disagreeable than ever. "They run around here like they own the place."

"Controlling cats is about as easy as herding butterflies," Viola said with a distinct twinkle in her eye. "And if they could speak, I believe they would tell you that they own *me*."

"You could sell this place and get yourself something

smaller and cozier, you know," Laura commented. "Isn't it far too big a house for one person?"

"Maybe for you." Viola regarded the younger woman for a moment. "I was raised in a big house and I'm not a small woman. Anything cozier would make me feel as if I were living in a closet."

Ted seemed impressed. "You don't feel lonely?"

Viola shook her head. "Being alone doesn't mean you have to be lonely, young man." She turned to Louise. "Do you remember that line you quoted to me once about loneliness? The one I wanted to embroider on a sampler and hang in the store."

Louise nodded. "It was one from C. S. Lewis. He said, 'We read to know we are not alone.'"

"There you go. As long as you have books, you'll never be lonely." She smiled at Louise. "Good friends certainly don't hurt either."

Chapter Four

When Louise and Viola brought the group back downstairs to tour the other rooms on the first floor, Ted commented on the unusual shape of the dining room, which started out as a rectangle but had two walls that projected out, forming a fifth corner in the center.

"I can't tell you why they built it this way," Viola admitted, "but I can tell people that I'm having dinner in the Pentagon and not be a liar."

"Are these sliding doors new, Miss Reed?" Edwina asked as she indicated the big walnut entry doors, which had slid away neatly into the wall between the hall and dining room.

"No, those are original to the house." She pointed to the opposite side of the room. "So is that swinging door over there."

"It leads to the kitchen, doesn't it?" Allan asked. When Viola nodded, he smiled. "A convenience for the servants, so they could use their hands for carrying heavy trays of food."

Edwina made a soft sound of surprise. "I never realized that was the reason for swinging kitchen doors. How fascinating."

The retired architect also pointed out the matching walnut wainscoting and window casing panels, which Viola said were in most of the rooms on the first floor. She turned to Laura, who was staring up at the ceiling. "You've noticed my chandelier, I see."

Everyone looked up to admire the hanging brass chandelier, the golden light from which reflected in the polished surface of her mahogany dining room table. Unlike typical chandeliers, it had no prisms or any glass at all except for the lights. Instead, it was formed from a single hoop of ornate brass, around which were spaced eight unusually scrolled brass supports. Out of each fluted end of the supports rose an artificial candle with a tapered bulb.

"I had that shipped over from England," Viola told the group. "The original chandelier was a fussy French thing with half the prisms cracked or broken, and as I'm not one for too much female frippery"—she gave Max a momentary, ironic glance—"I thought it would go well in here."

"Handsome fixture," he mumbled.

"Those scrolled holders around the edges look like little French horns," Laura said.

"They're real English hunting horns," Viola told her. "I found the fixture at an antiques auction I attended in London a few years back during a vacation. According to the papers that came with it, the chandelier originally hung in one of the faro rooms at White's Club in London."

"I've heard of that club." The interior decorator seemed very excited. "That's where Prince Charles had his bachelor party."

"White's Club has a bit more history to it than that," Louise said, her voice dry. "It dates back to the seventeenth century, when it was built as a place to serve hot chocolate, a popular new beverage at the time. It burned down once and then was rebuilt. It became arguably the most notorious, ah, gentlemen's club of its time."

"My friend Louise is being polite. They called it a 'gaming hall,'" Viola said, looking completely unrepentant. "The members of White's would write wagers with each other in a betting book that was always kept out on a table. They'd place bets on anything—births, marriages, government appointments, even deaths."

"Was that legal?" Edwina looked unwillingly fascinated.

"Probably not," Viola told her, "but it went on all the time. According to legend, a man fell unconscious in front of the door to White's. When they carried him into the club to get him out of the cold, the members began betting on whether he was dead or not."

Laura's eyes shone with intense interest. "Were you able to get anything else?"

"As a matter of fact, I picked up a pair of side lamps in the back parlor, which is where we'll go next."

Louise had always felt that Viola's back parlor was the

heart of the house, and not just because it contained her friend's excellent collection of classic literary first editions. The largest room on the first floor, it had been furnished and decorated specifically for the pleasure and contentment of an avid book lover.

There were three comfortable armchairs near the bookcases, which stretched from floor to ceiling along three walls. Four arched windows on the fourth wall allowed in natural light, while their heavy, ruby-velvet, portier drapes could be drawn to provide privacy. Two cats lay curled together as they napped amidst plump cushions of a sofa upholstered in rich, chocolate velvet.

Across from it was a matching brown sofa with a jewel-toned, Victorian crazy quilt throw draped over one end. Between the sofas sat a low, carved, cherry wood coffee table, the surface of which was inlaid with tiny, diamond-shaped slivers of paler wood that formed a geometric, interwoven design.

Viola's collection of first editions was extensive and filled several shelves of the bookcases. In what few spaces there were between the volumes, Viola displayed a number of interesting bookends, all shaped like animals.

"Now most of these pieces I inherited from my grandmother," Viola said. "In her day, they built furniture to last. Most of the books came from my father, who was a great reader and educated me thoroughly in classic literature."

"Are these the lamps you got at the auction?" Laura asked as she went over to one of the two reading tables by the sofa to admire the globe-shaped glass chimney of the elegant copper and brass lamp.

"They are," Viola acknowledged. "If you look beneath the globes, you'll see engravings of different game animals around the sides of the base."

Edwina went to have a look at the other lamp. "These side grips look just like little cats' heads. How charming!"

"Electric, but still," Louise heard the interior decorator mutter, as if to herself, "so *authentic* looking."

"These were originally oil lamps, weren't they, Viola?" Louise asked.

"They were. Whoever put them up for auction had already drilled and fitted them with electric wiring." She shook her head sadly. "A terrible thing to do to antiques of this quality, but it lowered their value enough that I was able to bid on them."

"It doesn't matter," Laura said. "I have to have them."

Viola's brows rose. "I beg your pardon?"

"I'll buy your lamps and that brass horn chandelier," the interior decorator said. She rummaged through her purse and produced a long, slim wallet and a gold pen. "I'll make out the check right now. Is it R-e-i-d or R-e-e-d?"

"It's n-o." The bookshop owner folded her arms. "What gave you the impression that I was selling them?"

"Oh dear, have I gone and rushed things?" Laura tittered a little. "Let me explain. I have a bachelor client who has just made a killing in the stock market. He hired me to make over his entire house for him and he was very specific about what he wanted—English antiques, but nothing frilly or fancy. He wants authentic, of course, so I know he would go crazy over these."

Viola shook her head. "I'm sorry, but you can't buy my lamps or my chandelier."

"I will pay you twice what they cost." When Viola didn't reply, Laura pressed her lips together for a moment. "Fine. I'll give you triple the price."

Louise cringed at the greedy sound in the younger woman's voice. *Does she not realize how crass she seems?*

"No, thank you."

Laura seemed unconcerned about what anyone thought. "I'll barely clear a profit, but I always go the extra mile for my clients."

"Is that so?" Viola went over and stood on the other side of the lamp. "Well, this time you'll have to go another mile to somewhere else, because I'm not selling them."

Louise thought that would be the end of it, but she had underestimated the thickness of Laura's skin.

"Surely with all your cats and your little bookshop, you could use the money," the interior decorator said, her tone less wheedling than before. "Particularly for your business. I mean, how many books can you sell in a town this size?"

Viola's cheeks flushed, a sure sign that she was going to lose her temper at any moment. "You're standing in my home, madam, not my business."

Madam was what Viola called women she disliked. To date, Louise had only heard her call Florence Simpson that, and only under extreme circumstances.

I need to put a stop to this right now, before the disagreement escalates any further. But what can I do? She gazed at the other visitors and then spotted Ted's camera.

"Ted, would you mind taking a photo of us?" Louise asked quickly. "Perhaps in the front parlor, by the Christmas tree? I am sure Miss Reed and the rest of the group would enjoy having a memento of this visit, if you can spare some copies. I know I would."

Ted had been taking photos and had evidently not kept up with the conversation. "But you said that you ... weren't ... ," he trailed off for a moment, moving his puzzled gaze from her to Viola and Laura, and then he nodded quickly. "Sure, I think that would be great."

"Laura, Viola, will you join us?" Louise asked. "We want to get everyone in the picture, naturally."

For a moment it appeared as if the two women were

not going to budge before Laura made an exasperated sound and stalked out of the library.

Viola turned to Louise and glowered. "You hate having your picture taken. You'd rather walk through deep snow barefoot on the way to church."

"That's true." She gently tucked her arm through Viola's. "But I enjoy spoiling a brewing argument even more."

"Pity," Max said as he passed by them, startling her. "Looked like it was going to be a good one."

When the group reassembled before the Christmas tree in the front parlor, Ted snapped several shots, pausing between each to ask Laura or Viola to smile. "Come on, ladies, there's no substitute for a happy face."

"Those lamps would be a start," Laura said. Her checkbook was still in her hand. "I'll never find anything like them." She released a breath of frustration. "Why did I think I would get anything out of this tour? The whole trip has been a waste of time."

A substitute, Louise decided, was just what the young woman needed.

"Not necessarily, Laura. Our next stop on the tour will be at the home of Joseph and Rachel Holzmann," she reminded her. "They own an antique shop and have a delightful selection of lighting fixtures. I'm sure they can help you find something suitable for your client."

"Personally I think you should buy reproduction lamps," Edwina put in. "They're much easier to obtain, less costly to replace if they're broken and far more reliable to operate. You should point that out to your client. Unless they're collectors, men usually appreciate practicality over aesthetics."

"Considering how many lamps I've broken in my lifetime," Allan said, "my wife would second that."

Viola nodded. "I've had to have the electrician over to fix the wiring on that old chandelier at least once a year since I had it put in."

The crimped line of Laura's mouth eased a little. "Wiring *does* lower the value of the piece."

"There are some very fine reproductions on the market," Louise added. "My sisters and I needed some additional lighting for our guest rooms when we remodeled our home. We were able to get all the lamps we needed for the same amount we would have spent for a single vintage piece."

"I've never shopped for them myself. Are you sure they don't look"—Laura made an uncertain gesture—"chintzy?"

"Not if you shop at the right place," Louise assured her. "If you are unhappy with what the Holzmanns have to offer, I can give you the name and address of the home furnishings shop in Potterston where we bought our lamps."

For a moment it looked as if Laura might come up with another argument, then she put her checkbook back in her purse. "I suppose I could have a look at it. If you change your mind, Miss Reed, let me know."

"I will," Viola said, obviously meaning it would be a warm day at the North Pole when she would. "If you'll all sit down and make yourselves comfortable, I'll bring in the refreshments."

Alice finished wrapping her Christmas gift for Louise—an ivory silk piano shawl with violets of velvet adorning the center panel—and tied a length of flat, eyelet lace around the box as an interesting substitute for a bow.

"There." She carried the gift to her closet and added it to the small stack of boxes inside. "That takes care of my big sister."

She studied the gifts for a moment, trying to think if there was anyone she had forgotten. She had purchased a lovely, hand-crocheted, chenille sweater in a deep mossy-green shade for Aunt Ethel from the same shop in Potterston where she had found the shawl for Louise.

For Rev. Kenneth Thompson, the pastor of Grace Chapel, she had selected a book on carpentry during biblical times, since he so enjoyed woodworking and the refinishing of furniture. For each of the girls in her ANGELs group she had made a beaded WWJD ("What would Jesus do?")

bracelet and a hand-painted wooden angel ornament for her family's Christmas tree. She would present the gifts after the girls finished their caroling trip around town that evening.

Alice liked to shop for other people more than she did for herself. She looked down at Wendell, who had come to investigate the open closet door. "I think I did okay this year. What do you think?"

Wendell showed his approval by making a beeline for the gift boxes, which in years past he had considered his personal scratching surfaces.

"Oh no!" Alice scooped him up and firmly closed the closet door. "I can't get away with claiming that the shredded-wrapping look is the latest thing again."

The tabby jumped down from her arms, gave a single, slightly disgusted look and stalked out of the bedroom.

For their other friends, Alice and her sisters were giving gift baskets like the one Louise had taken to Viola Reed. In each basket Jane had tucked two dozen assorted cookies and a loaf of Louise's aromatic fruit-and-nut bread. Alice had left the cooking to her sisters and had done her part by decorating the baskets with white ribbons, and red and green fabrics with snowflake patterns.

All she needed was one last gift, a gift for Jane, who had been insisting all month that she wanted nothing special for Christmas.

She should have something special. She needs *something special.* As Alice went downstairs to finish stapling the caroling booklets that she had made up for her ANGELs group, she thought of how busy Jane had been keeping herself.

Ever since the last of their guests had departed, her sister had thrown herself into hectic activity and had spent most of the day in the kitchen. She had already made so many cookies, candies and pans of fudge that her output could satisfy the entire town's sweet tooth. Alice could not recall the last time she'd seen Jane sit down for longer than two minutes.

"Lord, I hope it's only excitement and not something else." Alice went into her father's study, where she had been working at the desk, and sat down to finish the booklets.

Although the ANGELs went caroling from house to house each Christmas, this year's forecasts of colder temperatures and heavier snowfall made Alice decide to try something different. At their last weekly meeting, she had suggested that the girls perform in front of Town Hall. By doing so the girls could sing without having to tramp through the snow, and visitors as well as townspeople could enjoy the carols.

Clarissa Cottrell had generously offered to provide free hot chocolate and some of her beautifully decorated sugar cookies for the girls after their performance.

"I've been keeping the bakery open an extra hour every

night so I can catch up on orders," she had told Alice, "so it's nice and warm inside. Just send them over when they're through for their treat."

The red kettle one of the mothers had given her to use to collect donations after the performance was a little dusty inside, so Alice took it to the kitchen to wash it. There she found Jane sitting at the table, a mug and an open cooking magazine in front of her. Holiday music spilled from the radio on the kitchen windowsill, while two large pans of oversize brownies iced with a textured, golden brown mixture added the scent of dark chocolate and caramelized sugar to the cozy kitchen atmosphere.

The sight of her sister relaxing for a change made Alice's heart lighten. *Maybe I'm simply imagining things.*

"Can you spare a treat for your poor, overworked sister?" she joked. When Jane did not reply, she set the kettle in the sink and the sound it made caused her younger sister to jump. "I'm sorry. I didn't mean to startle you."

"It's only what I deserve for sitting here daydreaming." Jane came to join her at the sink, but her smile seemed a little dim. "What's this for? You're not having the girls bob for apples in this weather, I hope. They'll need to chip a hole in the ice first."

Alice chuckled at the image. "No, we're hoping to collect some donations after the caroling for our Christmas mission." As she filled the kettle with water, she gave her sister a sideways glance. "You were a million miles away when I came in here."

"Yes, and it was much warmer where I was. I want to go back."

Alice was not fooled by her casual explanation. "Something bothering you?"

"Nope." Her younger sister squared her shoulders and picked up two potholders in order to move the pans from the cooling racks to the table. "How about I ruin your lunch with one of these? They're German chocolate brownies with coconut and pecan frosting. Guaranteed to make your taste buds sing a Wagner aria."

"Maybe I'll have one for dessert." Alice turned off the water and added a squirt of dishwashing liquid to the kettle. In a nonchalant way, she added, "So what did you get Louise for Christmas? You never did tell me."

"A complete set of Peter Rybar and Marcelle Daeppen's classical duets on CD," she said. "He was a famous Czech violinist, and she was a pianist and his wife. I thought it might remind her of happier times, when she played duets with Eliot."

"I'm sure she will love it." She picked up the scrub pad and went to work on the kettle. "You always find the most unusual gifts for people, and yet they're so appropriate."

"That gorgeous piano shawl you found for Louise made me green with envy," Jane confessed. "The colors, the silk fringe, everything about it is just *so* Louise."

"I thought so too." She rinsed the soapy water from the kettle. "Christmas gifts should be special, don't you agree?"

"Absolutely."

"I think they should be tailored to people's tastes too. Like the shawl with Louise—you know she'll love that."

"Of course she will. She was admiring one just like it in a catalog a few weeks ago." Jane stopped cutting the brownies and looked at her. "*Uh-oh*, I've talked myself into a corner, haven't I?"

"Just a small one." Alice smiled. "You have been a bit evasive about what sort of gifts you'd like for yourself, you know."

Jane glanced back over her shoulder. On the wall over the kitchen table, Louise had recently hung a photo of Daniel Howard with the three of them when they were girls.

"Do you remember when that picture was taken?" she asked, nodding toward it.

Alice studied it. A very young Jane was dressed in a green velvet jumper and had her dark hair in tiny, lopsided pigtails tied with red ribbons.

"Yes, I think I do. That was at one of the Sunday school

Christmas parties. Father had Henry Ley dress up as Santa to take pictures with the children, but you flatly refused to go near him."

Jane frowned. "I'm trying to imagine myself being afraid of Santa—or Henry—and I'm failing."

"You weren't afraid. You told Henry straight out that you knew that he wasn't the real Santa because he didn't have any reindeer parked on the roof." She sighed. "The only way we could coax you in front of the camera was to let you sit on Father's knee instead of Henry's."

"I don't remember that," Jane said, her voice a little sad. "It seems like there are so many things I've forgotten or I missed."

Alice recalled a discussion during dinner with her sisters and Aunt Ethel several days earlier. They had spoken of Christmases Jane had only barely remembered. "Honey, did we make you feel left out when we were reminiscing the other night?"

"No, I love listening to your stories." Jane leaned against the counter and scrubbed at a nonexistent spot. "I miss Father. I miss having Christmas with Father, and you and Louise too. You know, I can clearly recall only about eleven of the Christmases I spent at home with the family."

"You counted them?" Alice had never done that and was a little disturbed to know that Jane had.

"When you're far from home, all you have are your memories." She shrugged. "It just seems like my childhood raced by in a flash and then it was over. So many Christmases since then have felt hollow and, well, pretty meaningless."

"Is that why you're working yourself into exhaustion every day?" She gestured around the kitchen. "Is this your way of trying to recapture those memories? The fact is we never spent all day in here baking."

"I know." She looked at the brownies. "I think I'm trying too hard." She met Alice's gaze. "I'm sorry."

"You have no reason to apologize," she said in her most comforting tone, "no reason at all."

Jane looked uncertain for a moment. "Do you really want to know what I want for Christmas?" When Alice nodded, she said, "It's something you can't buy. I want, so badly, to have that same, joyful feeling I had as a girl. I want good memories to outnumber the bad ones. I know it sounds greedy, but Alice, eleven Christmases weren't enough."

"You're not greedy." Alice went over and gave her younger sister a hug. "I promise that we'll make this Christmas Happy Memory Number Twelve."

Chapter Five

*L*ouise accompanied Viola to the kitchen, where she helped her friend prepare two trays with cups of nutmeg-sprinkled eggnog and plates containing small scoops of a dark brown, very moist-looking cake.

"It was good of you to provide this treat for our visitors, Viola," Louise said as she placed some folded paper napkins on the tray. "I also appreciate your help with the tour of the house. Even with the tour company's literature, I could never have told them as much about it and your family's holiday traditions as you did."

"I needed room in the refrigerator and I enjoy showing off for a crowd," her friend replied as she topped each portion of cake with a drizzle of thin, sugary glaze. "I must say I'm surprised to find you guiding a house tour. What got you involved with this bunch?"

Louise gave her a brief explanation of what had happened at the Coffee Shop. "I am trying to keep a good Christian attitude about it," she added, "but sometimes I wish my sisters would ..."

"Control their impulses?"

Louise laughed.

"Your patience never ceases to astound me. How do you manage people like that decorator woman?" Viola's tone went up an octave. "Where was she reared, in a designer *barn*?"

"I don't believe Laura meant to be deliberately rude," she said as she picked up the tray of eggnog cups. "Although I must wonder at her reasons for coming on a holiday home tour if all she intended to do was shop for her business."

"She's a troll."

That startled another laugh out of Louise. "Dear me, I don't think she is quite that bad."

"Not the *Lord of the Rings* kind of troll. A business troll. It's what my father used to call estate buyers who'd read the obituaries so they could be the first to make an offer to the heirs for the valuables of the deceased. They make large profits that way, especially if the family needs money fast. Some people call them hearse chasers."

Louise grimaced. "That sounds ghastly."

"It's more common than you think. Most people don't realize the value of their belongings, particularly if they're inherited. Along comes a troll and . . ." Viola rolled her eyes. "I imagine our decorator friend makes a good living buying antiques and such in that manner." She fussed for a moment over the arrangement of the plates on the tray. "Before I forget, you and your sisters are invited to my house for dinner on Boxing Day. One of my customers sent me a fully dressed goose, and Lord knows, I can't eat it all by myself."

Louise suppressed a smile. Viola always made her dinner invitations sound as if they were made only for her personal convenience, when she suspected the exact opposite was true. Despite her often brusque nature, Viola liked entertaining more than she would ever admit.

When the two women returned to the parlor, the tour group was discussing what they liked about the house and their own family traditions. All but Max Ziglar, who was standing by the bay window and looking out at the snow-covered garden.

Louise could not see his face and she hardly knew enough about him to guess what his thoughts were at the moment. In spite of this and his cantankerous personality, she had the strongest sense that the businessman was extremely lonely. *In this lovely, warm room, filled with all these friendly, interesting people, no less. What could have made him so determined to keep others at a distance if he doesn't like being alone?*

As they handed out the refreshments, Viola asked, "Has anyone ever had plum pudding before?" When some indicated that they had not, she added, "Before you try it, let me tell you something about it. This recipe was handed down to me by my mother and dates back three generations before her. English families have enjoyed plum pudding as their traditional Christmas dessert since the seventeenth century. I should also point out that the pudding has never once been made from plums."

"It smells delicious," Ted said, "but it doesn't look like any pudding I've ever seen."

"The original version was made of thick porridge, to which the cook added chopped meat, liquor, a variety of dried fruits, sugar, spices, butter and eggs. The mixture was boiled, not baked, in a cloth bag or special basin. Every member of the family took turns mixing the batter so that they could make a wish as they stirred."

The young man grinned. "Sounds as intriguing as the pudding smells."

As Ted lifted a large forkful to his lips, Viola cautioned, "Before you taste, mash it a little with your fork first, young man. The rest of you do the same. You might find a surprise."

"I've found something." Max prodded his portion with his fork. "It's sticking up out of the center."

"Ah, then you're the lucky one, Mr. Ziglar." Viola went over and used his fork to extract a bright silver dollar. "Another Reed family tradition. We throw coins, buttons, rings and thimbles into the mix."

"Edwina, would you like to have mine?" Laura asked after giving the bookshop owner a single, appalled glance. "I'm not really that hungry."

"Don't panic. They were a way to forecast the coming year. Whoever got the portion with a coin in it could look forward to wealth, a ring meant marriage, and those poor souls who found buttons and thimbles were doomed to stay single another year." Viola handed Max his plate. "I've never found a coin or ring yet myself. You're a fortunate man."

"I don't like *things* in my—" Max began, only to be interrupted by Edwina.

"Wasn't it Prince Albert who made plum pudding a standard during the holidays?" the schoolteacher asked hurriedly. "Or was it Charles Dickens?"

"Both, I think. Prince Albert contributed his part by being a little homesick," Viola said. "He grew up in Germany, and when he came to England he missed the traditions of his youth. The Queen pampered him by serving his favorite foods. That included plum pudding, which eventually was added to what had been the standard holiday fare of boar's head, wassail and mince pie."

"Boar's head?" Laura paled. "The whole head?"

Viola nodded, obviously enjoying the younger woman's reaction. "Have you ever had headcheese? Want to know how they make it?"

"Say no, Laura," Edwina murmured.

"*Ah*, what was done at court inevitably trickled down through society and was mimicked," Louise said, trying to draw them back onto the subject, "even by the poorest and humblest of families. Dickens, of course, popularized the treat in *A Christmas Carol*, where Mrs. Cratchit served hers 'blazing...in ignited brandy....'"

As the group finished their refreshments, Viola took a moment to admire the gift from the Howards, especially Louise's contribution, which was fragrant with the scents of ginger and nutmeg. "Thank you again for this, Louise. I'll look forward to having some of your nut bread in the morning with my coffee."

"You're welcome. If you find a silver thimble in one of the slices, give me a call." She chuckled at her friend's startled expression. "Wendell carried off mine from my sewing basket last week and I haven't seen it since. Maybe he decided to spice up my bread."

⌒

Louise preceded the tour van back to town, where the group was scheduled to break for brunch at the Coffee Shop for an hour before continuing on to the Holzmanns' home. She had to admit that the tour had gone better than she had expected, thanks in large part to Allan and Viola.

She was actually looking forward to taking them on to the next house.

As she parked, Louise sat in the car for a moment and watched the group climb out of the van. "All right, Lord. You were right, I was wrong. Being a Good Samaritan feels very nice."

Ted and Allan insisted on Louise's joining them at the Coffee Shop, and over their light meal of omelets and citrus salad they discussed Viola Reed's home and how intriguing Queen Anne architecture was in general.

"I'm fascinated by how surprising such houses are," Allan said. "Like Miss Reed's home—it's not a predictable structure, so when you first walk through you really never know what's going to be around the next corner."

"Rather like the owner, I imagine," Ted put in as he removed his glasses and cleaned the lenses with a paper napkin. "But at the same time I have the funny feeling that once you get to know her, you always know where you stand with that lady. Would you agree, Louise?"

Louise tried to think of a discreet way to describe her friend's penchant for blunt honesty. "Viola never minces her words."

"I picked that up right away," Laura said, apparently oblivious to her own lack of tact.

Allan stroked a tanned finger across his white mustache

in a thoughtful manner. "It's a shame that every year more homes like Miss Reed's are demolished instead of renovated and restored. Although some can't be saved, I've always felt as if I were watching history evaporate into thin air."

"History is for books," Max Ziglar said. "Houses should be efficient, practical and suited for life in modern times."

Louise was not surprised by his attitude. The businessman struck her as a thoroughly modern man. That immediately raised another question in her mind: *If he felt that way, what was he doing on a tour of historical homes?*

"History gives us a sense of place and purpose, by telling us from where we came," Allan said, taking exception to Max's statement. "It inspires us to create our own history for future generations. It's really no different than what we do as parents to set a good example for our children and grandchildren."

Max's gaze grew distant. "Then they grow up and do what they want."

"You can combine them, you know," Laura said. "Spread some bits of history around a modern house. That's what I do. People like both." Her cell phone rang, and she answered it with "L. A. Lattimer" before she rose and walked away from the table.

Louise privately wondered if anything really mattered to the interior decorator outside of making money. "What is your opinion on homes of historical importance, Edwina?" Louise asked.

The schoolteacher brushed a wave of her salt-and-pepper hair back from her round cheek. "I'm like Allan. I think history should be passed along to the next generation. Houses like Miss Reed's make excellent classrooms. I would love to have brought some of my students along with me." Edwina told them a little about the inner-city school at which she taught and added, "Most of the children live in apartment houses in the city and don't even have a yard where they can play."

"My father died when I was young and my mother could only afford an apartment after that," Ted mentioned. "Once you get used to the lousy maintenance, noisy neighbors and terrible views, they're not so bad."

Louise suspected otherwise and her heart went out to him. "Do you still live in an apartment, Ted?"

"For the time being. My wife and I fell in love with an old Colonial-style farmhouse that we discovered outside the city." He took out his wallet and removed a photo of the house and showed it around the table. "As you can see, it needs some renovation, but it stands on fifteen wooded acres. It's really the sort of place you dream about owning."

"Have you put a down payment on it yet?" Edwina asked.

"Our present incomes keep us from qualifying for the home loan we would need, but"—he shrugged again—"we'll keep saving our pennies to buy it or something like it."

Jane helped Alice load her car with the gifts for her ANGELs and with a box of caroling booklets. Before Alice drove off, Jane promised to meet her sister in town as soon as she finished a few last-minute chores at home. "I am not going to be late, I promise. I really want to hear the ANGELs sing."

Alice studied her face for a long moment. "All right, but remember, I'm counting on you."

As soon as she heard the car drive off, however, Jane left the kitchen and went into Daniel Howard's study.

Whenever she felt troubled as a child, she had come to this room. Her father had always kept his door open, even during the afternoons when he worked on his sermons, and he had always made time to listen to her. When her father was not at home, Jane would still visit his study and sit in his favorite armchair, and feel instantly better.

She needed that kind of comfort now.

Jane had not been entirely honest with Alice earlier when they had talked about Christmas. She did miss the happy holidays of her childhood, but that was not the whole problem. Jane was not even sure what was driving her to such hectic activity. She only knew that she felt better if she kept busy from dawn until dusk.

I'm trying too hard, she thought.

She should have thought, *I'm running away from this vacation*.

Jane moved around the room, running her hands over the backs of chairs, looking at the different photos Daniel had displayed of his wife and daughters. Although her father was gone and the room had been redecorated, she still felt his presence whenever she came into the study.

A photo of Daniel and his daughters captured her attention. She studied it, looking into his kind eyes, wishing she could reach into the photo and touch his hand.

"I wish you were here, Father." She went to his favorite armchair and curled up on it. "I could really use your advice."

Daniel Howard had always known how to talk to her. He had coaxed her to talk about her concerns simply by helping her to sort out her feelings. She could remember a dozen times when she had rushed to the study, looking for him.

"I'm not going to school today, Father," she had once said when she was in the fifth grade, "I'm never going to school again."

"Come here, Jane." He had set aside his Bible and taken her onto his lap. "You're feeling very angry today, aren't you?"

"Yes. I'm so angry I could blow my top, just like a volcano."

"That's not a very good feeling, is it?"

"No." She had buried her face against his chest. "I hate being angry. It hurts my heart."

"So you're feeling a little sad, then too. Were you sad before you felt angry?"

She had not meant to tell him, but the words began pouring out of her. "No, I was angry first, when Will and Jerry made fun of me on the way home from school...."

Now Jane slowly began to sort through her feelings, asking herself the same questions that her father would have, trying to pinpoint what she had not been able to express to Alice.

Like her sisters, she had wanted this Christmas to be special. She had not lied to Alice when she said that. She also understood Louise's reluctance to get involved with the tour group. They had gone to a lot of trouble to arrange the time off in order to be together for the holidays and do all the things that they never had time to do.

Yet on the first day of their long-anticipated vacation, Jane had talked her sisters into giving up some of their time to help guide the Christmas homes tour. She had told herself that it was the Christian thing to do, but there was a small corner of her heart that was glad to give up some of the time with her sisters in order to spend it with people that she did not know. People who did not know her. People who really did not care about her. People who had no expectations where she was concerned.

That was what confused her. That same little corner of her heart wanted to find other things to do. Things that would keep her occupied and busy. Ways she could use up the time when she might otherwise be idle.

No, she had to be brutally honest, at least with herself. She wanted to find things to use up the time that she had promised to spend with her sisters.

Jane knew that Alice had expected her to go with her to town, and yet she had used chores as an excuse to stay behind. If she had gone in the car, Alice would have wanted to talk more about Christmas and gifts and how much fun they were going to have. And she did not want to do that. She did not want to keep up a happy pretense.

Would she really rather scrub the kitchen floor than spend time with her sisters? Part of her said yes, because it was easier to be busy. It was safer. Like pretending not to want anything special for Christmas.

There were a dozen things Jane might have suggested, but she was worried she would ask for too much, or the wrong thing. She did not know what they expected of her.

"I don't want them to be disappointed in me." Was

that what she dreaded most? She was avoiding their time together and keeping so busy so they would have no reason to complain about her or to feel resentment toward her.

She had rarely come home for Christmas before, when their father was alive, and now she would never have another Christmas with him.

Jane closed her eyes. Of course, that was the root of it. She was acting out of guilt.

Stay busy, don't ask for anything special and no one you love will have any reason to resent you.

Daniel would have let her cry and then he would have prayed with her. Now she would have to pray by herself, and in that moment she missed her father more than any other time since his passing.

"Dear Lord," she prayed, "You gave us this beautiful holiday, and here I am, spoiling it. Help me with my feelings. Help me to accept the love my sisters have for me instead of being afraid of it. And if You have some extra all-purpose courage lying around, I could sure use some."

Chapter Six

*A*fter the group had enjoyed a relaxing meal, Louise led them in the minivan to the next stop on the tour, the German Inglenook bungalow owned by Joseph and Rachel Holzmann.

Some of the oldest oak trees in town were on their property, and their solid presence complemented the simple lines and sturdy construction of the Holzmanns' house.

A wide, overhanging eave created by the extension of the main roof protected the white front porch. The porch itself was spacious enough to accommodate an old-fashioned porch swing, two rocking chairs and a wicker patio set without giving the impression of being crowded.

It was the sort of home where one could imagine himself on a lazy July afternoon, sitting on the front porch swing, sipping a glass of cold lemonade and simply watching the clouds roll by.

"This time I would like to read something aloud from the literature your tour company sent to me," Louise said as she extracted a folded paper from her purse and opened it. "Mainly because I have not memorized it."

Ted laughed. "We won't give you a test, later, Louise. Honest."

"Thank you, Ted." She consulted the paper. "'The word *inglenook* is made up of two words: nook, which means seat or corner, and *ingle*, which comes from the Gaelic word *aingeal* for fire or light. Combined, they indicate a corner or place by the fire.'"

"I'm all for a place like that," Edwina said, shivering a little.

Louise folded the paper as she nodded toward the uppermost section of the Holzmanns' roof. "You can see that the house has a chimney in the very center there. I'm no expert, of course, but I do know that Inglenook homes were always built around their central fireplace."

Ted studied the front wall. "It seems so modern-looking."

"A Craftsman home was, for its time." Allan walked up to the front porch and scanned the front of the house, which had three sets of large windows on the first floor and a row of smaller, clerestory windows above the wide porch roof. "I wasn't sure from the literature, but this is a classic Gustav Stickley design. Quite an impressive example at that."

Louise was beginning to realize how fortunate she was to have a retired architect along on the tour. Allan Hansford's knowledge of house design was nothing short of remarkable and did much to round out her own limited presentation.

"It only looks like a little ranch house to me," Max said, clearly unimpressed. "What's so historic about it?"

"Stickley was a leader in the Arts and Crafts movement, and he popularized it through his designs," the retired architect explained. "The standard of the last part of the nineteenth century had been ornate Victorians, like Miss Reed's home, but Stickley chose to build furnishings and homes that were clean, practical and no-nonsense."

"You called it a 'Craftsman' home. What does that mean?" Edwina asked. When Laura made an impatient sound, she added, "Well, I know it didn't come from Sears."

"It was Stickley's own term for his individual style, although the generic term typically used for his furnishings is 'mission furniture.' Gustav Stickley had a wonderful maker's mark too. He would sign each piece with a sketch of a medieval joiner's compass and the phrase *Als ik kan*, which means 'as I can.'"

"Nice motto," Ted said. "Although today it would probably be 'when I can.'"

The architect chuckled as he walked up to the front door to study the dark wood frame. "You're right, Ted."

"Allan, thank you. You have saved me at least fifteen minutes of reading from the literature, for which I'm sure everyone else is grateful," Louise said as she walked up to the door to ring the Holzmanns' bell.

"I thought it might be you folks. Welcome," Rachel said as she opened the door to usher everyone inside. "Come in, come in. I'm Rachel Holzmann and my husband Joseph is around here somewhere."

Louise made introductions, but the visitors were already taking in the Holzmanns' large front living room, which was a showcase for their private collections of antiques and Christmas decorations.

The sweet, spicy smell of the air came from clove-studded orange pomanders hung from the boxed ceiling beams. A tall, full Christmas tree redolent of fir occupied one corner by the fireplace and glittered with ornaments in a rainbow of colors. A comforting warmth emanated from a blazing fire on the natural-stone hearth, and on the other side of the room, an archway led directly into the informal dining room.

"We put out a few things for the holidays," Rachel said, giving Louise a smile.

That was an understatement of epic proportions. Being antique dealers who were devoted to their field, Rachel and Joseph had impressive collections displayed all around the house.

Louise watched with pleasure as the visitors looked around them with wide eyes as they took in the framed botanical prints; a hutch filled with collections of colorful spatterware, redware and graniteware; and the open baskets and mason jars filled with smaller items, like old glass buttons, cat's-eye marbles and advertising thimbles.

"I am dying of curiosity about one thing already," Edwina said and pointed toward the front door. "Why do you have the letters *C*, *M* and *B* written in chalk above your doorway, Mrs. Holzmann?"

"That is an old custom my parents taught me. When I was a girl, they would inscribe the initials for the Three Kings, Caspar, Melchior and Balthasar, in order to invite God's blessings on our home." She turned to the rest of the group. "This is the first year my husband and I have participated in a Christmas homes tour, and I have a little presentation I'd like to give. If I may steal the spotlight from you, Louise?"

"Please do." She was happy to relinquish it.

"Joseph and I bought our home about twenty years ago. To tell you the truth, when we first looked at this house, I thought I'd walked into another time zone. Outside it was bright and sunny. Inside it was dark, dark and more dark." Rachel went to one wall and indicated the wood paneling, which was stained the color of roasted chestnuts. "The original stain was actually darker than this. Back-of the-bear-cave blackish-brown, I called it."

"You were not a fan of dark woods, I take it," Allan said, underscoring the obvious.

"I was used to the interior style of our previous home, a modern Italianate house with painted plaster walls and ceramic tiling. I told my husband that visiting this house was like leaving Venice to lose oneself in the Black Forest." She paused as everyone laughed. "You can understand then why I was prepared to rip out every bit of wood or paint it white. Happily, Joseph bought me a book on Stickley homes and made me read it first."

"Thank heavens," Allan said. "Dark as it is, you have a real jewel of a house here, Mrs. Holzmann."

"We like to think so." Rachel retrieved an old magazine from a side table, which she passed around to the group. "The plans for our home were published in this issue of *The Craftsman*, a magazine Stickley published, which, as you can see, is dated 1910. The previous owner's grandfather, a wool merchant by the name of Karl Schroeder, worked directly from the plans when he built this house."

"Then the house is much older than it looks," Edwina said.

"The Stickley Craftsman has been the baseline for nearly all the bungalow designs since the original," Allan said. "It has never had time to become dated. Karl Schroeder made a very good choice."

"There is a portrait of Karl and his family on the wall above the fireplace, by the way." Rachel pointed to the framed, sepia-tinted photograph, which showed a short, bearded man wearing glasses; a plump, fair-haired woman wearing a pretty muslin gown; and three identical-looking tow-headed boys in knee-length pants.

"Are those boys triplets?" Edwina asked. When Rachel nodded, she murmured to Louise, "God bless Mrs. Schroeder."

Rachel swept her hand toward the hall. "If you'll follow me, I'll show you the rest of the rooms."

The first floor of the low-slung bungalow also contained a master bedroom, guest room and kitchen, as well as what Rachel referred to as their "work and play room." It contained her sewing machine, a card table and Joseph's work bench.

"The built-in cabinetry in the dining room and kitchen is original to the house, and is made from oak trees grown right here on the property," Rachel told them. "Because Stickley homes were usually built by their owners, instead of by contractors, making use of local materials was common. That further defined the individuality of these houses, as a Craftsman home built in California from the exact same design plan as ours might have redwood cabinetry and a slate stone fireplace."

Rather than remove the original features of the home, Rachel explained, she had combated the dark colors by providing light prints and paintings, mirrors and a *trompe l'oeil* mural, which so closely resembled a window opened to overlook a flower garden that Louise imagined she could almost smell the realistic-looking pink roses.

"Our second floor originally had four bedrooms and a bath, but for the convenience of our guests we converted one of the bedrooms into a second bath." Rachel took them to see the renovated room, which she and Joseph had decorated to look exactly as it would have at the turn of the century.

"How original," Laura said, making notes on her electronic planner with a stylus. As she wrote, she kept lifting her gaze and darting it around, as if she did not know what to look at next. "How did you find all these things?"

"We're in the antiques business, and the renovation of this room started when Joseph found this wonderful, old claw-foot tub at a dealers' show in Atlanta," Rachel told her. "It was in mint condition—a very rare find in period plumbing fixtures, I should add—and we decided to buy it and then build the bathroom around it."

"But these aren't all antiques," Laura said, tapping the sink with her stylus. "This looks far too new."

"It's a reproduction. Part of our business is to find fixtures to complement a specific antique piece, like our porcelain tub here. Often our clients specifically request reproductions, especially if they're going to be subjected to regular household use."

"That's a good selling point," Laura said and looked up from the device she was using. "What is your standard mark-up on reproductions? Do you use manufacturers or distributors? Oh, and do you ship direct or keep things warehoused for pickup?"

The flood of questions seemed to puzzle Rachel. "Are you in the antiques business, Laura?"

"I buy them now and then," Laura said, suddenly putting on a coy expression. "Just little accessories for the houses I do."

Edwina rolled her eyes at Allan, who only shook his head.

Louise reined in a sigh. "Perhaps business questions could wait until after the tour."

"Come by the store if you have a chance tomorrow," Rachel suggested. "I'll give you one of my cards when we go back downstairs. Joseph and I are always happy to talk shop with someone in the business."

That seemed to please Laura. "Thank you, I will."

Through one of the upper-floor windows, Rachel showed the group the small barn at the back of their property, which she and Joseph now used as a garage, and then they returned to the first floor.

"What amazed my husband and me most when we searched through the original estate papers was how little it cost Karl to build this house." Rachel swept a hand around. "Care to take a guess?"

Ted guessed four thousand dollars and Laura said five. Allan went lower with fifteen hundred and Edwina suggested two thousand.

"Seven hundred," was Max's guess.

"You're very close, Mr. Ziglar. By trading work and materials with other merchants, Karl built all this for less than five hundred dollars."

"Good Lord. That's what my wife and I pay for one month's rent on our apartment," Ted said. He gazed around the house and sighed. "Why couldn't I have been born back then?"

"Average wages at the time were probably only a couple of dollars a week." Edwina patted his shoulder. "So it wouldn't do you any good to make that wish."

"I'm beginning to think all my wishes are pretty foolish," the young man admitted. "Art is beautiful, but like Max says, it doesn't pay the bills."

Louise felt her own heart ache for the young man. She had always considered herself fortunate for being able to live her dream of becoming an accomplished pianist. She had never thought of what life would be like if she had been denied that.

Ted obviously loved photography, but he was trapped in a job where he was forced to use it for minimal pay according to the whims of others. Louise imagined it would be the same if she had been forced to play the piano in a club or at children's birthday parties, just to make a living.

Please, Lord, she prayed silently, *let him find success with his gift before his dreams are gone*.

Chapter Seven

*J*oseph Holzmann came in through the back of the house and greeted everyone. In his arms he carried a stack of firewood, which he took into the living room to deposit by the fireplace before returning to meet with the group.

"Were you related to Karl Schroeder, Mr. Holzmann?" Edwina asked after introductions were made. When Louise gave her a surprised glance, she added, "I notice a certain resemblance between you and the portrait of him."

"You're very perceptive. Karl was my grandmother's first cousin," he said, hanging up his heavy coat. "His family and hers immigrated together here to America just after the Civil War. When his granddaughter decided to sell the house, she put the word out to family members first. As Rachel and I had our hearts set on moving to the country, we came to have a look at it. It was all downhill from there."

"It was the best decision we ever made," Rachel said, beaming at her husband.

Joseph took his turn as guide by telling them of the German immigrants who had started coming to North

America in the late seventeenth century and how many of them had chosen to settle in Pennsylvania.

"German immigrants wanted big, solid houses and preferred to build within their own communities, with wood and quarried stone versus the usual brick and plaster." Joseph brought out a photo album with old photos and postcards that he and Rachel had collected over the years, and showed them some examples of the homes that the immigrants had built. "This was also a practice of Dutch immigrants, whose homes were likewise considered enormous by colonial standards of the time.

"Both the Dutch and the Germans fell in love with Pennsylvania. I think it reminded them of the open countryside where they had been brought up. According to the 1990 census, nearly forty percent of all Pennsylvanians today are of German descent."

"*Hmm*. How about those horse-and-buggy people?" Laura asked. "Are they descended from the Dutch settlers?"

The antique dealer shook his head. "The Amish and Mennonites trace their roots back to Germany, but they were misnamed the 'Pennsylvania Dutch,' probably because they spoke German, which in their language is *Deutsch*."

The Holzmanns took the group to see their Dutch-style back door, which was divided in half horizontally.

"I imagine the lady of the house would work on the laundry in here," he told them, "and open the top half to let in air while keeping the bottom half closed to keep her children in or the yard animals out."

Next they took the group back to their front living room, where Joseph explained the changes Karl Schroeder had made to the alcove brick fireplace from the Stickley plan by using a wider, deeper hearth and quarried granite rock left in its natural state.

"The benches are based on built-ins from the original design, but Karl created extra storage room by enclosing the bases and hinging the seats to double as lids." He raised one to show them the firewood he had stored inside. "Traditionally Germans put their fireplaces in the center of the house. This was to take advantage of heat distribution and because the hearth was the center of home life. They not only cooked here, but they bathed and read by firelight as well."

Max's eyebrows went up. "They took baths in the living room?"

"In the winter it was the warmest spot in the house," Louise said. "There were no hot water heaters in those days, so the water had to be heated on a stove or over an open fire. Better to bring a tub by the fire than haul buckets of hot water up the stairs."

The Holzmanns invited the group to sit and discuss any questions they had about the house. All the guests were amused when Rachel stated that the only serious modification to the house that her husband had allowed was to screen in the rear porch.

"I learned to live with all this wonderful old wood and stone," she admitted, "but I drew the line at bugs in my lemonade."

"She can be awfully fussy that way," Joseph said, teasing her.

"I really admire all the antique collections you have around the house," Edwina told her. "The way you display them is fascinating."

Louise also liked Rachel's inventive ways of displaying their possessions. Instead of keeping them segregated in cabinets and on shelves, she had them out in different, ingenious arrangements that showed them off while making them seem like a perfectly natural part of the room.

"You're actually sitting right next to Rachel's largest personal antique collection," Joseph told her, nodding toward the tree, which the firelight made glitter brightly. "She's become such an expert on German blown-glass ornaments that I'm trying to convince her to write a book on them."

"I'd rather spend the time hunting down more ornaments for my collection," Rachel said as she went over to the tree and gently traced her fingertips over a blown-glass version of Santa Claus. "I do love them, though. My father was a glassblower who made laboratory-grade glass containers, and one of my happiest memories as a girl was going to the glassworks to watch him."

Rachel explained that blown-glass ornaments had been made as far back as the sixteenth century, originating in the eastern part of Germany and then quickly becoming a major industry that spread through the country.

"The first blown-glass products that were made weren't ornaments, but ordinary household items like drinking glasses and serving bowls. It wasn't until the Christmas tree become popular in the nineteenth century that artisans began producing *kugels* or *kugeln*, which were simply balls of silvered glass, like this one." She took a silver sphere from the tree to show them. "My ancestors worked in glass factories in Lauscha, which my father considered the birthplace of ornament art."

"Why is there a pickle hanging on your tree?" Laura asked, wrinkling her nose as she peered at it. "Is that something German too?"

"Ah, you have very sharp eyes. Yes, that's another family tradition. The pickle ornament is always the last one to be hung on the Christmas tree. My parents would hide it after my sisters and I had gone to bed on Christmas Eve, and whoever found the pickle in the morning would be the first one to unwrap his or her presents."

"What do you get if you find a sauerkraut ornament?" Allan teased.

"You get to make a Reuben sandwich." Rachel chuckled. "You would not believe how often my sisters and I knocked our heads together, searching the tree for that pickle."

"It must have been hard to find too." Allan admired the little ornament, which was life-sized and molded to look exactly like the genuine article. "Seeing that it's the same color as the tree."

"They are very pretty ornaments, but storing them must be a nightmare," Laura said.

"You simply have to take some extra care with them," Rachel told her. "Glass ornaments should be individually wrapped in acid-free paper and packed in a sturdy, sectioned, single-layer box. The biggest mistakes people make are heaping them together, letting them roll around loose, or wrapping them in plastic or bubble wrap."

"It was easier to deal with decorating a tree before the introduction of glass ornaments," Joseph added. "Glass of any era needs proper ventilation. If you store your ornaments in a basement or attic, you should keep them in a dry, dark spot away from light, dampness and extreme temperatures."

"I'd like to do a lesson plan about glass ornaments when the children come back from Christmas vacation," Edwina said. She had been discreetly writing some notes on a small pad. "Do you know what the German people used to decorate their trees before glass ornaments, Mr. Holzmann?"

"Sometimes small gifts were tied to the branches with ribbon," he told her, "but mostly people decorated with edible items like cookies, candy, nuts and dried fruit."

Edwina grinned. "So you didn't have to pack up ornaments after Christmas. You could just eat them."

"I think I could handle that," Ted commented.

Laura wandered over to a shelf displaying a row of unusual-looking frames and boxes made of layered and carved wood. "I've seen these before in some magazines. They're called hobo work or something like that, aren't they?"

"The official term is tramp art, but examples that Joseph collects are ones specifically made by German immigrants. We dealers refer to their craftsmanship as chip-work or edge-carved," Rachel said. "Since this is Joseph's particular area of expertise, I'll let him tell you about it."

"My wife is being diplomatic. She's heard me complain too often about how maligned tramp art has become in the last fifty years," her husband said. "The pieces I collect were made by traveling German immigrants and are unique to the Pennsylvania area."

"They appear to be made out of little bits of wood," Allan said as he studied a picture frame.

"Edge-carved pieces are almost exclusively made from scraps of wood and from cigar boxes made of wood. Those pieces were very popular during the period after the Civil War right up until the Great Depression. That was also a period when cigar smoking was very fashionable. Often itinerant workers would trade finished pieces for food, lodging and discarded cigar boxes from which they could make more items."

"That must have been tedious." Despite his observation, Max seemed truly interested. "How did they use the cigar boxes?"

"The carver would cut down the old cigar box wood into thin strips, which he would glue together in layers, in a pyramid fashion." Joseph took the lid from one trinket box and held it up to the light. "Once he formed a solid object, he would use different methods of carving to further define and decorate the edges, and to give an illusion of depth. Edge-carvings are some of the oldest examples of American folk art."

"I love these miniature crèches," Edwina said, admiring the tiny Nativity scenes that the Holzmanns had displayed on the mantel above the fireplace. "What did they use to get such fine details?"

"Edge-carvings were simply made by hand with a whittling knife," Joseph told her.

Ted bent to look at another shelf. "These look like toys."

"Animals and other children's items, which we call whimsies, were almost as popular as picture frames and treasure boxes," Joseph acknowledged. "Noah's ark was a favorite theme." He picked up an intricately carved cane resting against one shelf. "Walking canes were another specialty. I have a client who collects only edge-carved canes."

"I think it looks too busy." Laura pursed her lips. "I've seen better."

Although that made Louise take in a sharp breath, Joseph didn't take offense. "A lot of people think of edge-carvings as too gaudy or kitschy. Since a small amount of it was made by anonymous hobos who used the railroads to travel the country, many antique collectors consider it cheaply made, but this is a misconception."

"Is it?" The interior decorator seemed amused by this. "What makes it so special?"

"The majority of edge-carvings were made by immigrant itinerant workers and *wanderburschen*, or traveling apprentices, men skilled in the art of wood carving." He turned over a picture frame to show her where the slivers of wood joined in hundreds of tiny joints. "You can imagine the painstaking work that went into fashioning just this one piece. Edge-carving may be a 'working class' art form, but it really doesn't deserve its bad reputation."

"Why did these men wander around the countryside when they could have settled down somewhere?" Ted asked as he raised his camera to take a photo of the collection.

"Most Germans came to America in search of jobs, but

they found only seasonal work on farms. Single men who didn't have families would travel quite a bit to search for work. Their craft was often called tramp art, a term that was not considered a derogatory one during their time period, by the way. It was literally what they had to do to earn a living—tramp about the countryside on foot, looking for work."

"If they'd only found a good woman to marry," Allan said, "they'd have settled down and saved a lot of the wear and tear on their shoes."

"That reminds me, I have to show you my little 'bride's tree,'" Rachel said and disappeared into the dining room for a moment. She emerged with a miniature fir tree, upon which tiny glass ornaments were hung. "These are our very first ornaments, given to me by my mother on the day I married Joseph. There are twelve ornaments, and each has a symbolic religious meaning to help ensure a happy life for the newlyweds."

"They're so small, like dollhouse ornaments," Edwina mused as she admired the little tree. "Do you know the meanings for the different symbols, Mrs. Holzmann?"

"Let's see if I can remember them," Rachel said and started to point to each one. "The angel is for God's guidance, the rabbit for faith and hope, the teapot for hospitality, the house for protection and shelter, the rose for affection, the bird for happiness, the basket of fruit for generosity, the flower bouquet for good wishes, the pinecone for mother-hood, the fish for God's Blessing, the Santa for goodwill—"

"And a heart for true love," Joseph said, coming over to give his wife an affectionate kiss on the brow.

"Could you stay that way for just a second?" Ted asked as he backed up to take a photo of the Holzmanns and their bride's tree.

Unfortunately, he was so engrossed in adjusting the dials of his camera and looking through his lens that he didn't see the table behind him.

"Ted, please, stop!" an alarmed Louise called out as he came too close to the edge.

It was already too late. The table tilted and fell over with a crash.

Chapter Eight

W hat the . . . oh no." Ted whirled around and nearly dropped his camera as he surveyed the mess.

Everyone looked horrified except for Rachel, who came over and put a hand on the young man's shoulder, wanting to ease his embarrassment.

"It's all right. See?" She bent and picked up a four-inch-tall wooden nutcracker, which was not broken. "You picked the right table to bump into, young man."

"Mrs. Holzmann, I am *so* sorry," he said, blushing as he crouched down to help her pick up the old toys that had been scattered. "I'm afraid I see the perfect shot and the rest of the world vanishes."

"It's a beautiful camera you have there." She righted the table. "Are you a professional photographer?"

"Not yet, but I'm hoping to make it my profession." He picked up an overturned bowl, set it on top of the table and began placing other nutcrackers in it. "If I could publish photographs of places like your home, Mrs. Holzmann, it would give people all over the country the opportunity to take a tour like this and never leave their armchairs."

"If you ever want your own home, Venson, you'd better stick to a regular job," Max said. "You'll never get a steady income selling pictures, however pretty they are."

Louise winced at the particularly unpleasant note in Max's voice and how eager he was to take every opportunity to discourage the younger man from pursuing his ambitions. *He must have sacrificed his own dreams long ago.*

After the table had been rearranged, Louise asked Rachel if Jane had been to her store lately.

The antique dealer frowned. "No, Louise, I can't say that I've seen her since, *hmm*, August I think. Why do you ask?"

"I am trying to find a Christmas gift for her, and I was hoping she might have stopped in and shown some interest in something at your shop."

"When Jane has come to the store, it's always to buy gifts for others. She never splurges on anything for herself." Rachel gave her a sympathetic glance. "I wish I could recommend something, but I'm afraid I don't know your sister well enough to do so."

"I'll think of something," Louise said. "Thank you anyway, Rachel."

They finished the tour with a round of thanks from the group and a promise to stop by the Holzmanns' shop in town.

"*Gesegnete Weihnachten und ein glückliches neues Jahr,*" Rachel said as she showed them out the front door. "A blessed Christmas and a Happy New Year to you all."

⌒

As the sun began to set, shoppers hurried to make their final purchases before the shops closed in Acorn Hill. The end-of-the-day bustle was cheerful as the tired but satisfied merchants happily rang up sales and wrapped parcels, and their customers delighted in reducing the number of items left on their shopping lists.

Instead of going home, as they usually did, most of the shoppers and shopkeepers lingered downtown, gathering in a loose crowd in front of and along the sides of Town Hall. To help keep cold hands warm, June Carter had set up a little concession stand selling hot drinks and Clarissa Cottrell's fresh donuts.

Everyone was waiting for Acorn Hill's ANGELs to give their Christmas performance.

Inside the Town Hall, Alice handed out caroling booklets and made sure all of her young performers were wrapped up warmly in coats, mittens, scarves and hats. "Now girls, don't be nervous. Remember what Pastor Ley said about not rushing the songs, and try to smile and make eye contact with the audience. If you think you can't smile, just look at me. That should do the trick." The girls laughed. "I am very proud of all of you for all the hard work you've done preparing for this performance. Is everyone ready?"

The girls chorused a resounding "yes," and Alice chuckled as she led them out to take their positions in front of the audience. Parent volunteers handed out battery-powered electric candles to each girl, and when they were assembled, the tapered bulbs lit up each small face with a lovely, warm glow.

"Ladies and gentlemen," Alice said, "thank you for joining us this evening. The ANGELs of Grace Chapel have a wonderful selection of traditional carols to perform for you. We'll begin tonight with 'Go Tell It on the Mountain.'"

Alice stepped to the front of the crowd and turned to face her young charges. She lifted her hands to signal the time to begin and the young girls' voices blended together in harmony.

All around them, proud parents, townspeople and delighted visitors listened to the time-honored songs of the season. Alice felt a familiar pang in her heart as she watched the girls. They had practiced these songs for weeks, at every meeting, and it showed in the very polished performance.

The ANGELs' shining eyes and happy expressions were reflected in the faces of the crowd by the time they reached the final stanza of the last carol on their program, "O Holy Night."

Truly He taught us to love one another,

His law is love and His gospel is peace.

Chains He shall break for the slave is our brother

And in His name all oppression shall cease.

Sweet hymns of joy in grateful chorus raise we,

With all our hearts we praise His holy name.

Christ is the Lord! Then ever, ever praise we,

His power and glory ever more proclaim!

His power and glory ever more proclaim!

For several moments after the last, sweet voices hushed, everyone was silent. It was then that Alice felt the presence of the Lord so strongly. Lifting up praises to heaven with song was such an integral part of Christian life, but the Christmas season had its own, very solemn significance. There was no better way to honor the birth of Jesus Christ than through the voices of the children He had taken on human form to save.

After the pause, enthusiastic and appreciative applause made the girls' faces flush. Parents came forward to claim their daughters for hugs, and offered their own heartfelt praise to the children and to Alice. The outpouring of approval, as well as Clarissa Cottrell's reminder to drop by the bakery for hot chocolate and sugar cookies, made the ANGELs' smiles widen.

Before the girls left with their parents, Alice distributed her little gift bags and asked the youngsters to join hands for a short prayer.

"Dear Lord," Alice said, "In this holy season when we are given so much, do not let us forget the many gifts and blessings You bring into our lives. Help us to remember that Christmas is a celebration of the birth of Your Son, Jesus Christ. Remind us to be grateful for our friends and families, whom we so often take for granted. We thank You for the beauty and peace of this holiday, for giving us the voices to reach into each other's hearts and up to heaven with our praise, and for filling our lives with joy of worship and fellowship. You are the way, the truth and the life, now and forever, through Christ our Lord. Amen."

The ANGELs then surprised Alice by presenting her with their own Christmas gift, a scrapbook that they had made, filled with photographs and handwritten descriptions of what their group had done since the previous Christmas. Each girl had made her own pages, and they had all met after school to work on the book together.

It was the loveliest present Alice had ever received from the girls, and after thanking them and joining in an affectionate group hug, she sent the girls off with their parents to have their treat at the bakery.

Jane, who had come to hear the girls sing, came to her side. "It's too cold out here for you to be crying," she said. "The tears will come out like little ice cubes."

"Heaven forbid." Alice rubbed a gloved hand over her eyes. "Were you able to finish up your chores?"

Jane nodded. "I want you to know that I am clearing my schedule from here on out. No more marathon baking or house-cleaning sessions. This is our vacation, and I'm going to spend it with you and Louise."

The note of determination in her sister's voice puzzled Alice. "If you want to have fun baking things, you go right ahead. This is your vacation too."

"Don't encourage me." She tucked her arm through Alice's. "In fact, if you could drag me out of the kitchen more often, I'd appreciate it."

Alice was about to ask why when she saw Louise's car. "Oh, look, there's our big sister." She waved at the car.

They returned home together, and over a late dinner that evening, Alice and Jane listened to Louise's report on her experience guiding the tour group.

"I must say that Viola and the Holzmanns were extremely helpful by providing so much information about their homes," Louise said after they cleared the table. "I would not have had as much success without their assistance. Alice, when you take the group to Mayor Tynan's home tomorrow, you should ask Lloyd if he would do the same."

"You can ask him now," Aunt Ethel said as she came through the kitchen door, followed by the mayor. Both were carrying old-fashioned berry baskets filled with various baked goods wrapped in holiday-patterned cellophane. Their aunt took the basket from her beau and handed both to Jane. "Just put these out of reach before he sneaks something else, like he did on the walk over here."

"I did not sneak anything," Lloyd said, looking very self-righteous.

"Crumbs," Jane murmured as she passed by him and tapped the right side of her lips.

The mayor hastily brushed the betraying bits of pastry from the corner of his mouth, but the damage had been done. "Now, Ethel, you know I can't resist your cooking." He patted his ample waistline. "However much I wish I could."

"You can work it off by helping the girls decorate their tree tonight," their aunt said firmly, then turned to Alice. "Were you able to bring down the ornament boxes from the attic?"

"Yes, Fred helped me carry them down earlier when he delivered the tree." She grimaced. "I think some of the glass balls might have been broken when we were moving things around in the attic. I distinctly heard the sound of broken glass rattling about in a few of them."

The sisters, Ethel and Lloyd adjourned to the reception area, where Fred had set up their impressive Douglas fir in a tree stand. Alice began passing out boxes from the neat stacks in one corner.

"*Uh-oh.*" Jane made a mournful sound as she looked

down into the box she held. "Anyone have some instant-bonding glue and a heck of a lot of patience?"

Louise suggested they check through all the boxes first, and to their relief all of the antique ornaments they had inherited from their parents were still intact, thanks to careful wrapping and the old, heavy boxes they had been stored in.

The boxes of the glass ball ornaments they had purchased more recently, however, had not fared as well in their flimsier containers. Most of them had cracked or broken.

"It's not Christmas unless you break something," the mayor said, trying to cheer them up.

"Then it's going to be Christmas for another twenty years," Jane said, ruefully surveying the damages.

Lloyd helped Jane dispose of the boxes of broken ornaments, while Louise, Alice and Ethel began unwrapping the ones that were still intact.

"I should have ordered a smaller tree," Alice said, feeling a little intimidated as she looked from the decidedly shorter stack of ornament boxes to the enormous tree. "I don't think we have enough left to decorate it properly. I won't be able to use any of these for my wreath, either."

"We can improvise and make up some ornaments of our own." Louise described the way Viola had decorated the greenery around her home with ribbons and fruit, and then added, "The tree is only for family this year, so no one should object." One side of her mouth curled. "Unless you want to invite Max Ziglar to the house."

"I hear that man is more depressing than rain on a Sunday," Ethel put in, "when he's not harassing that nice young man who has been taking all the photos."

Louise regarded their aunt. "How *do* you manage to gather your information so quickly?"

Ethel produced a small, satisfied smile. "I'll *never* tell."

"Is he really as irritable as he looks?" Alice asked. She would have to deal with Max the next day, and from all the accounts that she had heard, she was not looking forward to it.

"I am not sure that he is." Her older sister took a beaded apple ornament from one box and attached a wire hanger to it. "He does tend to be very gruff and gloomy, and to criticize Ted about his desire to be a professional photographer. I have yet to see much that has pleased him. However, I have the feeling there is a very deep-rooted sadness in him."

"If he's depressed why would he come on this tour?" Alice asked.

"I can't say for certain, but . . ." Louise shrugged. "My thought is that he came because he is tired of being alone, but doesn't know how to be anything else."

"He's missing his business and his money, more like," Ethel said. "I told you."

Jane returned without Lloyd.

"Our mayor insisted on making us his special-recipe hot chocolate," she told her sisters and aunt. "I tried to argue him out of it for two seconds and then caved in. I think it was watching him get out the saucepan. I love men who aren't afraid of pots." She glanced at Ethel. "What's this about money and why would anyone miss it?"

"I was talking about Max Ziglar and the way wealthy men behave."

Jane nodded. "Big man, unhappy eyes."

"He gave Louise a hard time today and he's got too much money for his own good." Ethel plucked an ornament hanger and hooked it to a gleaming blue glass bird. "Wealth makes you unhappy and dissatisfied with everything."

"I don't agree," Louise said at once. "Look at the Holzmanns. They are quite wealthy and yet they are a generous, happy couple who genuinely care about the community."

"Rachel and Joseph are exceptionally good people, I'll grant you that," Ethel said. "But this Ziglar man is never going to be like the Holzmanns."

"You're not giving him much of a chance, Aunt," Jane said. "People can and do change, all the time."

Alice did not want to jump to conclusions about Max, either. "He might improve on better acquaintance."

"I ran into that group in town today," their aunt told them. "Their driver had brought them from the Holzmanns' to do some last-minute shopping in town, but that rich man didn't want to stay."

"Men usually don't like to shop," Alice said.

"I heard him tell that skinny woman that he wasn't interested in buying gifts for anyone." Ethel sniffed. "What sort of man says that at Christmastime?"

"Maybe there is no one in his life." Always the champion of the underdog, Jane jumped to his defense. "He might not have a family, and lots of wealthy people have trouble making friends."

"Ebenezer Scrooge had friends once," their aunt said darkly. "Look at how he behaved."

"He also found redemption," Alice felt she had to point that out.

"Exactly, Alice. Max might just be depressed about being alone during the holidays and he's dealing with it by being scrooge-ish." Jane turned to her. "I think you should try to cheer him up. Treat him like one of your crankiest patients at the hospital."

"Somehow I don't think Mr. Ziglar is going to let me give him a foot rub," Alice deadpanned.

Lloyd brought in a tray of steaming mugs. "Jane, I nearly got lost in your pantry. But if I ever do, I won't starve for at least two years."

Feeling suddenly chilled, Alice paused to pull on a sweater before she accepted one of the hot cups. "I should adjust the thermostat, it seems like it's getting colder in here." She breathed in the dark, spicy scent of the drink before she tasted it. "My, this is very good, Mayor. Not like any hot chocolate I've ever tasted."

"An old family specialty. I'll give Jane the recipe, if she can guess what I put in it," Lloyd teased.

"Let's see now." Jane carefully sampled hers. "Baker's chocolate, milk, a touch of vanilla, cinnamon and . . . ," she took another sip before adding, "ground cloves?"

The mayor laughed. "You win."

The front door opened, and Alice turned to see Fred and Vera Humbert walk in. They were smiling but looked very cold. "Did you happen to make enough for two more cups, Mayor?" Alice asked.

"Coming right up." Lloyd went back to the kitchen.

The Humberts shed their snowy coats and handed over a parcel, as well as a Christmas gift basket filled with apple butter, spiced pears and Vera's special homemade vanilla fudge as they greeted the sisters.

"Fred told me he was coming over to drop off some replacement Christmas bulbs Louise had ordered, and I thought I'd come along to bring our gift basket now, before the weather gets worse," Vera said.

"Are we due for a storm?" Jane asked.

"There's a blizzard in the works," Fred told her. "The temperature's been steadily dropping, and we've been getting more wind than usual. All the animals are holed up in their trees and dens too." The store owner was also an amateur prognosticator and often made predictions about the weather based on signs from nature.

Alice and her sisters had never really taken Fred's weather predictions very seriously, until one summer day when he had correctly predicted a violent storm. While Fred was not always one hundred percent accurate with his forecasts, they tended to listen to him more carefully now.

"Will it be a dangerous storm, Fred?" Alice asked as Lloyd returned with hot chocolate for the Humberts.

"I don't know about that, Alice," he said, "but I believe we'll definitely be seeing a heap of snow before Christmas arrives."

"You said we'd be hit with four feet of snow at Christmas a few years back, Fred," Lloyd reminded him. "That didn't pan out."

"True enough," Fred agreed. "But this time the signs are much stronger. I haven't seen a bird or squirrel or rabbit for two days, and animals always sense these things. I'd bet money on it this time, if I were a gambling man."

"It won't hurt to stock up on a few things, just in case," Alice said.

"It's a good thing you girls took time off," Ethel said. "You don't need guests to deal with along with a snowstorm."

Chapter Nine

*T*he next morning Alice left bright and early to meet the tour group at Town Hall, where she escorted them inside to meet the mayor.

Lloyd Tynan came out of his office accompanied by Fred Humbert, who greeted the group before going over to a ladder set up beneath an overhead light. Alice suspected that he had been drafted to install the new bulb that he carried since the mayor was not quite as nimble as his friend Fred.

"Before we go over to the house, I'd like to tell you a little about the history of Acorn Hill," the mayor told the group and proceeded to show them through the Visitors Center. "And this year we have a special display, made by none other than our local hardware store owner—and lightbulb-changer extraordinaire—Fred Humbert."

Fred smiled down from on high, then quietly turned his attention back to maintaining his balance.

Lloyd glanced over at Fred, who had begun his descent. "Fred," he called out, "do you have a minute to show the folks what you've done for the holidays?"

Fred consulted his wristwatch. "I can spare a few minutes before I have to be at the store."

Alice was surprised to see that Fred had set up two incredibly detailed model train layouts of different sizes.

It's like I've been transformed into a giant, she thought as she looked down on a model of snow-covered hills and a picturesque valley town.

The train set that Fred had assembled possessed the exact detailing that made it an authentic copy of the real thing. Allan Hansford experienced a moment of nostalgia for the trains that had traveled near his home in his youth.

Ted crouched down to take a photo of the layout. "Do you set up model trains at home, Mr. Humbert?"

"When my daughters were little, I'd always have a train layout of some kind set up for them," Fred said as he bent to switch on something beneath the model. Tiny electric lights sparkled all over the model. "Alice, would you push the little blue button by the mailbag pole?"

Alice did so, and the entire model went into motion.

In the village, traffic and car lights blinked. Windows in the ceramic houses and shops lit up. A horse-drawn sleigh moved on a hidden track from town to a farmhouse, jingling bells all the way. The church's tiny doors opened and the choral sounds of "O Come, All Ye Faithful" drifted out. On a mirror serving as a frozen pond, little children skated figure eights around each other.

Fred scanned the rapt faces around the table and then grinned. "It's not as impressive as the big layouts they have over at the model train museum, but I like to go for quality over size."

"I wish my dad could see this," Ted said as he changed positions to take another photo from a different angle. "You'd never get him out of this room."

Fred seemed pleased to hear that. "After the holidays I was thinking of setting up the trains as a permanent display in my store. If you're ever back in the area, you're more than welcome to stop by with him any time."

"You mentioned a museum, Mr. Humbert. Where is that, exactly?" Edwina asked.

"Well, ma'am, we've actually got two train museums in this region. The Train Collectors Association, of which I'm a member, operates the National Toy Train Museum. Then you have the Railroad Museum of Pennsylvania, which has more than a hundred full-size, antique locomotives and boxcars they've restored and preserved. Both of them are in Strasburg, just west of here."

"Now I know where you sneak off to whenever Vera goes to the Amish markets," Alice teased.

"Model train collectors like to congregate regularly," he admitted. "It's a hobby that encourages friendships, as we like to trade ideas and swap cars, tracks and so forth with one another. We can share it with our kids, too, which isn't something you can do with a lot of grown-up hobbies." When the bells from the Methodist church began to chime the hour, he glanced at his watch. "I hate to show off and run, but I do need to get to my store."

Everyone thanked Fred and bid him good-bye as he struggled into his coat and left the lobby.

"Grown men, playing with toys," Max grumbled, but even his eyes were drawn to the fine detailing.

"How long has your family lived in this region, Mayor?" Ted asked after he had taken several photos of the various other displays in the Visitors Center.

"I'm the third generation Tynan to grow up in this town and the fourth member of a Tynan family to be elected to the office of mayor." Lloyd curled his hands around the edges of his jacket lapels and regarded the display with pride. "You could say the Tynan family has always had an interest in community leadership. We've certainly never been shy about stepping up to serve the people."

"I would have thought a man like you would move to the big city, where the politics get really interesting," Allan said.

"I do enjoy politics, but I'm just a small-town boy at heart, Allan. Here, before I forget." Lloyd handed out town guidebooks to everyone. "These will help you get around if you're out to do some shopping."

Alice thought the mayor had come a long way from the man who once had insisted, "Acorn Hill has a life of its own away from the outside world and that's the way we like it."

"Is there anything else you folks need to know about the town before we head over to the house?" Lloyd asked.

"I can't smoke at the hotel or in any of the restaurants or homes on the tour," Max complained. "Is there anyplace I can have a cigar in peace?"

"You can always step outside to smoke, but I can't guarantee the peace," the mayor told him and nodded toward Alice. "My dear friend Miss Howard here will give you a good talking-to on what smoking does to your lungs and heart. She convinced me to give up my pipe many years ago."

Alice tried to keep her expression smooth when Max swiveled to glare at her. She generally avoided confrontations over matters of health.

"I'm sure you know how bad it is for you, Max," she said gently. "Also, breathing in secondhand smoke can create health problems for the people around you."

"It always makes my allergies flare up," Allan said.

"Smoke gives me a headache," Edwina added.

"You can save the lectures. I've already heard them all."
Max patted the pocket in his jacket where he kept his cigars.
"I can wait until I get home to smoke. I've waited this long."

That could explain his irritability, Alice thought. "Perhaps after
a few more days of not smoking, you might not want to."

As the minivan took the group from Town Hall to the
mayor's home, Alice gave Lloyd a ride in her car so they
could discuss how to handle the tour.

"Ethel was over the other day, telling me to dust all my
collection frames and whatnot, but my furniture and holiday decorations are pretty basic," he told her. "I hope they
won't be disappointed."

"You have a wonderful home," Alice assured him. "If
you could help me out with the finer details of its history
and so forth, though, that would make the visit more special for the group."

"I'd be happy to." The mayor glanced at her. "Ethel mentioned that you and Louise are a little worried about Jane."

"Nothing escapes my aunt, does it?" She shook her
head. "She's been working herself into exhaustion, baking
and doing things around the inn. This vacation was supposed to be so that we could relax a little."

"Active people have a hard time doing nothing," Lloyd
observed. "Your aunt can be that way too. I get my exercise
just trying to keep up with her."

Alice chuckled. "She is a bundle of energy, isn't she?"

"When you're older, staying busy can make you feel young," the mayor said. "When you're feeling sad, it can keep you from dwelling on bad memories."

Alice had never considered it from that perspective. "I think I do that myself sometimes."

"Of course, I'd be happy to be a professional couch potato, if I could find someone to pay me for the privilege." Lloyd chuckled. "As for Jane, I'd let her be, Alice. That's what I do with Ethel when she gets that way. Takes her a little time to work it out of her system, but then she always comes around."

Lloyd Tynan's house was only a short distance from the heart of town, and occupied a cleared tract of land ringed by elms and willows. Those trees, he told the group, had been planted by his grandparents when they had first arrived in Acorn Hill.

"My family roots are spread out all over New England and Pennsylvania," Lloyd explained as the group gathered on the front lawn. "I'm of Irish and English descent, with a bit of Scottish on my mother's side. My father's family moved here in the 1800s, and we Tynans have lived in this region ever since."

From the front the house appeared to be a plain, rectangular box of red brick with a small, built-on enclosed porch that sat on the left side. The front had four large windows and six smaller ones, each flanked by white sliding shutters. Separate doors indicated two entryways, and two chimneys rose on opposite ends of the steep, tiled roof.

"The house was originally built to serve as a meeting house," Lloyd said as he led them up to the left-hand door. "My grandparents were dedicated Quakers and my grandfather led the local congregation for many years until they disbanded during the Depression."

"How did your family end up converting the meeting house into a home, Mayor?" Allan asked.

"My grandfather bought the meeting house and land from his society, as he couldn't bear leaving the area," Lloyd told him. "I also think he had it in his mind that the Quakers would return someday, although they never did."

"Quakers were like that funny-looking man on the oatmeal box, right?" Laura asked.

"Quakers were a Puritan sect who referred to themselves as 'the Society of the Friends' or simply 'Friends,'" Alice answered. "They built their own churches, which they called meeting houses." She took out the literature from the tour company to glance at as she presented the information on the historic aspects of the house itself. "Mayor Tynan's home is one of the oldest examples of a nineteenth-century, two-cell meeting house still in existence."

"I'm putting in papers to have it declared a historic landmark," the mayor added.

Alice pointed to the different architectural features as she read them from the paper. "It has two stories and was built to be symmetrical, with each side of the house mirroring the other, as you can see from the twin front entries and duplicate sets of windows."

"Why is everything doubled?" Laura asked. "It almost looks like a duplex."

"In a way, it was," Alice affirmed. "Quaker men and women met together for worship, but separated for business discussions. In other words, boys on one side, girls on the other. This is more evident when you see how the inside of the house is arranged."

"But what made you decide to live in a *church*?" Laura asked the mayor, still perplexed.

"I grew up in this house, so I never thought of it as anything but my home." Lloyd unlocked the front door and opened it. On a wall just inside was a large, beautifully decorated, dried-flower wreath. "Come in and I'll show you why."

The interior hall split off in two directions, but opened up in the center into an enormous living room. Lloyd opened a closet near the entry to hang up everyone's coats and scarves before leading them into the big center room.

Allan pulled out a handkerchief just in time to catch a sneeze.

"God bless you," Alice said.

"We're in the right place for that," the retired architect said, making Lloyd chuckle.

"What sort of services did they have here?" Edwina asked as she looked around.

"The Friends used this house for many things, from worship meetings to business to educational classes for their children," Lloyd told her.

"What a nice little tree," Edwina said, smiling at the four-foot pine Lloyd had displayed on one table. "I really like your wreath too."

"My secretary made the wreath for me. I don't have a great many Christmas decorations, I'm afraid. My grand-parents followed the Friends' beliefs and didn't celebrate Christmas," the mayor told her. "They taught my father to spend the day bringing food and firewood to poor fami-lies in the community. My mother and father joined a different Christian congregation after they were married, but they too felt the holiday should be celebrated simply and with reverence."

Lloyd's decor was equally uncomplicated and gave the immediate impression of being tidy, but geared toward the comfort and taste of a bachelor. The furnishings were functional, with a variety of plaids and autumn-colored fabrics and drapes. A large primitive painting of a woman in Quaker dress hung in the place of honor above a fireplace and a pair of bookcases held an interesting selection of books on political history.

The mayor was quite proud of the two prayer benches placed near an antique wood-burning stove in the corner opposite the fireplace, which he identified as being original to the house.

"My parents installed plumbing and electricity for convenience, but I only use the central heating when it's really cold outside." Lloyd looked down at himself ruefully. "I come with plenty of my own insulation and I've always preferred a good fire during the winter."

The tour of the rest of the house went well as Alice and Lloyd led the group through the different rooms and identified each by the way the Quakers once used them. The mayor showed them where the elders and overseers met, and the side room used by women for their business meetings. He related how his father as a boy would listen in on meetings with other children in the upper gallery.

"Why did the Quakers call this a meeting house instead of a church, Mayor Tynan?" Edwina asked when they returned to the central living room.

"The founder of the Quakers, a man by the name of

George Fox, encouraged the Friends to meet wherever they could and not worry about the formal trappings of established religions," he told her. "They never really went public with the locations where they met either, as they were very private people."

"So it was a top-secret meeting house," Ted said, looking intrigued.

"In some ways, it had to be," the mayor agreed. "Secrecy became imperative when the first Quakers began being persecuted by members of other, opposing religions in power. Often they could avoid being arrested and having their property confiscated only by meeting away from their homes in places like barns or warehouses that could be simply converted for their needs."

"It's a shame they were treated that way," Edwina said. "Why didn't they fight back?"

"Quakers have always been dedicated to peace, ever since they first formed their religion in 1660," Alice told her.

"Weren't they over in England?" Laura asked.

"The religion originated in that country," Alice said. "In the mid-nineteenth century there was a split between Quakers in England and those in America that would last over one hundred years, partly because of itinerant ministers in Pennsylvania who spread a more evangelical message than the more mystic-minded Friends in England were prepared to support. American Quakers believed in a strong Christian doctrine and performed outreach whenever they could through different forms of social activity."

"Quakers were very different from other Christians, weren't they?" Ted asked.

"Until this century, it was quite easy to identify Quakers by their habits," Alice told him. "They were a splinter group, after all, but they had no qualms about showing the differences in their beliefs. Quaker men did not believe in 'hat honoring' and would not remove their hats, even in situations where every other man in the room would. Like our Amish friends, they believed in plain dress and would not wear anything but black garments without lapels or buttons, as colors and accessories were considered vanities. Most noticeable was their use of *thee* and *thou* when speaking, and their identification of the days of the week and the months by numbers instead of by the names we use."

"I've heard that the Quakers were very much against music and dancing," Edwina said. "Why was that?"

"Most forms of music and dancing were considered to represent extravagance and ostentation, two things the Quakers preferred to avoid. Also, there were concerns about regulating contact between men and women. They did allow some forms of music, but dancing was definitely frowned on." Alice smiled. "I don't want to give you the wrong idea about them. Quakers have always been very kind and devout people. It's true that their beliefs were strict, but they have always been deeply involved in charity work."

"Betsy Ross, the patriotic seamstress who helped to create the American flag, was raised as a Quaker," the mayor added. "I remember reading how she would bring food to the poor as a little girl."

"That reminds me that Mayor Tynan has a wonderful collection of political memorabilia here at the house," Alice said. "I believe you will find it just as interesting as the Quakers."

"Do you have a specific type of memorabilia you collect, Mayor?" Allan asked.

"My collection consists mainly of campaign pins, buttons and badges. I have a few really old ones, plus at least one example from each of our American presidents dating back to 1864, when President Abraham Lincoln ran for re-election in the middle of the Civil War." Lloyd took down a single frame and handed it to the schoolteacher. "This is my rarest specimen, a pin given out by the election committee to re-elect Lincoln."

Alice joined in admiring the one-inch-square pin. Inside a bronze-colored metal frame was an oval sepia-colored portrait of the beloved president. "Why is there a little hole at the top?"

"That was for a ribbon," Lloyd said. "The ribbon was then pinned to your lapel."

"Couldn't they just have stuck a pin on the back?" Laura asked.

"They figured out how to do that about fifty years later, Laura," Lloyd told her.

"Was it your family's involvement in local politics that made you begin your collection, Mayor Tynan?" Edwina asked.

"To tell the truth I never set out to collect them at first. My father was quite active in regional political campaigns, and whenever he came back from a convention he would always have a number of badges as souvenirs. It was my good fortune that he gave them to me." Lloyd picked up a wooden box and opened it to show that it was full of Pennsylvania state campaign buttons. "One of my friends boasted that he had gotten a presidential campaign button from an uncle who lives in Washington, DC, so I asked my father how I could get one of those. Father had me write a letter to the presidential election committee, and they sent my first one to me. I was so impressed that they would take the time to send a badge to a child who couldn't vote. From then on I was completely hooked."

"How much can this stuff be worth?" Max asked as he peered at a framed celluloid button with two portraits and the inscriptions "McKinley and Tanner" and "Illinois 1896."

"That one you are looking at there is worth about forty-five dollars on the collector's market. My Lincoln pin is worth quite a bit more, probably close to a thousand."

Laura squinted at the lone pin. "For this little bitty thing? Incredible."

"I don't sell them, but I've been known to swap some on occasion." Lloyd indicated the other framed groups of badges on the wall. "A lot of them I picked up at antique shows, but many were given to me by friends and colleagues. Alice's aunt found some wonderful old pre-World War II campaign buttons at thrift stores. I've also worked for several presidential campaigns myself and was able to obtain badges from them."

"Why do you limit your collection to pins and badges?" Laura asked. "Why not other things?"

"With all the campaign items today's candidates hand out—hats, T-shirts, bumper stickers and such—I'd never find the room to display them." He lowered his voice. "I'm also not much of a fan of dust catchers, if you know what I mean."

Edwina uttered a laugh. "Spoken like a true bachelor."

"So who invented the very first campaign button, Mayor?" Allan asked.

"Why, our very first president, George Washington. He wore a button to his first inauguration in 1789. I'm afraid I don't have one in my collection, but according to my collectors' guides it was a garment button made of brass and had the slogan 'G.W. Long Live the President' on it."

He showed them the oddest of his campaign buttons, such as the Andrew Jackson button with Jackson's signature on the back, and the celluloid watch fob upon which was a likeness to Theodore Roosevelt. Alice thought the strangest campaign slogan was that of President Harrison, who used a "born in a log cabin" motif on his badges, while in reality he had never lived in one but had been born in a large house to a wealthy, privileged family.

"What would a collector regard to be the rarest political campaign button, Mayor?" Ted asked.

Lloyd thought for a moment. "That does change a bit from year to year, as old badges are discovered in attics and so forth, but I would have to say the most prized badge is the one for James Cox from the 1920 presidential election."

"James Cox?" Edwina looked puzzled. "I've never heard of him."

"Most folks haven't. Cox buttons are rare since few were made compared to those for other campaigns. James Cox's claim to fame was really his running mate for vice president, a young, fairly unknown fellow by the name of Franklin D. Roosevelt."

Everyone chuckled over hearing that, even Max Ziglar.

Alice noticed that Laura had wandered away from the group and was crouching next to one of the prayer benches by a pot-bellied woodstove. She went to join her. "Is everything all right, Laura?"

"I'm fine." She stood up. "How long do you think these benches are? Three and a half feet?"

"Closer to four, I believe." Alice frowned. "Why do you ask?"

"Your sister tried to prevent me from doing business with Miss Reed yesterday." Laura gave her a too-bright smile. "I'm going to make an offer to the mayor for these and I'd appreciate it if you'd keep out of it."

Chapter Ten

*A*lice felt a sinking sensation in her stomach as she watched the interior decorator walk over to speak to Lloyd. Laura Lattimer seemed quite determined to get what she wanted, even if it meant creating a fuss.

Luckily, Lloyd was still telling the rest of the group one of his longer, amusing presidential anecdotes, so Laura had to wait to get his attention.

Alice still had a chance to solve the problem—if she could think of a way to divert the interior decorator from the objects of her desire. If Viola Reed had had trouble convincing the woman that she was not interested in selling her family heirlooms, then gentle, good-natured Lloyd did not have a prayer.

Lord, if You could inspire me with an idea right now, I would be eternally grateful, Alice silently prayed.

A few moments later the front door opened and, like an answer from heaven, Ethel Buckley entered the house carrying one of the Howards' gift baskets.

"Your sister sent me over because you forgot this back at the inn," her aunt said as she came to join her. "So?" She glanced at the group surrounding Lloyd. "How is it going?"

"Fairly well, with one exception. I need some advice." Alice drew her out of the group's hearing and swiftly explained the problem with Laura Lattimer and the prayer benches. "It's almost as if she promised to make a scene if I say anything. But if I don't do something, I think she might try to talk Lloyd out of his family's prayer benches."

"It sounds like she is already trying," Ethel said, scowling, as she nodded toward the group. "What nerve!"

Alice looked over and saw that Laura was now standing beside the mayor, speaking rapidly and gesturing in the direction of the living room. She even had her hand on his arm.

"Here, Alice." Ethel handed her the basket. "Let's go and give Lloyd his gift."

"It would mean so much to my client, Mayor," Laura was saying as the two women went over to stand near Lloyd. "He's a very religious man, a former preacher, I believe. He would be overjoyed to have the benches for the little Bible studies he holds at his home."

Obviously uncomfortable, Lloyd tugged at his collar with a finger. "I'm sure he would, but—"

"I would be sure to tell him all about the history connected to the prayer benches. I know he would preserve them with the utmost care," the interior decorator assured him.

Alice stepped forward with the gift basket, intending to speak, only to receive a quick, unpleasant look from Laura.

Lloyd valiantly tried again to make a polite refusal. "I do appreciate that, but I think—"

"You know, I want to recommend this tour to my business associates," the interior decorator said, her tone growing frosty, "but I'm starting to think the people in this town don't like outsiders."

As Lloyd hastily assured the young woman that she was mistaken, Ethel said to Alice in a low voice, "I'll be right back."

"What are you going to do?" Alice whispered back, worried now that her aunt might do something reckless and cause the confrontation she had hoped to avoid.

Her aunt was watching Laura. "I'm just going to put my purse in the living room." With a smile, Ethel went around the corner into the living room.

What on earth is she doing? Alice wondered. She stepped back to look at Ethel, who was taking something out of the corner of the mayor's wood bin, in which he kept his firewood neatly stacked.

"Alice?"

She nearly jumped as she turned to see Ted aiming his camera at her.

"Smile," the young man said just before he snapped her photo.

A moment later Ethel reappeared.

"Should I say something?" Alice whispered. She saw that the mayor seemed to be wavering.

"I don't think that will be necessary, dear girl." Her aunt headed toward her beau and Laura.

"You know that we give feedback comments on the tour to the company that runs them, don't you?" Laura was saying to Lloyd. "I do so want to say something really wonderful about Acorn Hill so that they will keep you on the circuit." She gave him a sly nudge. "Selling me those benches would certainly inspire me to lavish praise."

"Are you *finally* getting rid of those awful old benches, Lloyd?" Ethel asked as she came to his side.

Alice blinked. Maybe she'd heard her aunt wrong.

"The benches?" The mayor seemed equally confused. "Well, I, er—"

"It's about time," Alice's aunt told the group, sounding very matter-of-fact. "Who wants them?"

"I do." Laura lifted her chin. "I have the perfect buyer for them."

"You're the interior decorator, aren't you?" Ethel introduced herself and shook the younger woman's hand in a businesslike fashion. "Can you take both of them?"

Laura slanted a coy look at Lloyd. "If my offer is acceptable to the mayor, I'd be delighted to take them off his hands. At once."

"Wonderful. Thank you." Ethel turned to her beau. "Now Lloyd, before you take her check, you should really have Fred take a look at the termite damage and see what he can do about it."

Alice frowned. *Termite damage?*

"I'm sorry," Laura said. "Maybe we're talking about a different set of benches."

"No, he only has one set." Ethel gave Laura a sympathetic smile. "I know how you antique buyers love that distressed look in the wood, but you wouldn't want them to collapse the first time your buyer sits on them."

The benches were certainly old and the varnish on them had darkened, but Alice hadn't noticed anything wrong with the wood.

"I don't know what you're talking about." Laura marched back into the living room and pulled one of the benches away from the wall.

Alice came to stand beside her and saw little particles of wood on the floor where the benches had stood—particles that were, as it happened, the same color as the interior wood of the benches.

They were also the same color as Lloyd's firewood.

The interior decorator bit her lip as she bent to peer beneath the bench seat. "Is it . . . extensive?"

"Oh, those two moldy old things have been riddled with the little pests for years," Ethel assured her with a casual wave of her hand.

"Have they?" The younger woman stared.

"Lloyd has sprayed them with insecticide and plugged up the little holes they made, but you know how hard it is to kill termites once they've set up house in something. They always eat their way back out."

"Ah yes." The interior decorator straightened slowly. "Well, Mayor, under the circumstances I think I'd better withdraw my offer. Naturally I can't sell antiques that are . . . infested with something."

"I understand completely. Sorry that I can't help you." Lloyd looked as if he wanted to grab Ethel and whirl her around the room, but he settled for giving her a heartfelt kiss on the cheek. "How is my best girl today?"

"Just fine." Ethel beamed. "I thought that when you were finished with this tour, we could spend a little time together." She tucked her arm through his. "You owe me lunch, you know."

"That I do," the mayor agreed.

Ethel squeezed his arm, and then rubbed her palm

against the side of her slacks. A few tiny pieces of wood drifted to the floor. When she caught Alice watching her, she dropped her right eyelid in a slow, deliberate wink.

 ⌒

After Lloyd thanked them for visiting his home, Laura insisted, before getting into the minivan, that the driver leave the group in town for an hour so that she could visit the Holzmanns' antique shop.

"I don't like to be rushed into buying anything," she said, "and we only have one more day here before we go home." She took out her electronic planner. "There was a snow globe I saw in the window of a shop here. I have to have that for one of my clients, a collector. If only I can get the shop owner to bargain with me."

Alice found it ironic that the interior decorator liked to haggle over prices and have time to decide on her purchases, but she did not extend the same courtesy to those from whom she bought. She did not comment, however. Since leaving Mayor Tynan's home, Laura had been acting as if she was spoiling for a fight and Alice was not going to be the person to give her an excuse for one.

I'd better warn Jane, though, she thought.

As luck would have it, nearly all in the group indicated

that they had some additional Christmas gifts to buy, so Alice decided to tag along to see if she could find something suitable for Jane.

That is, until Max made his objections known.

"I don't need to spend any more money than I already have," he told the group. "I'd rather go back to the hotel now than spend all afternoon tromping through shops."

"I *want* that snow globe," Laura said. "If I wait another day, someone else will buy it."

"I'm not making two trips," the driver said. "Either I take my lunch break now and we go back in an hour, or we go now and I take it at the hotel."

"Max, it's just an hour," Edwina said. "Why don't you go and have some coffee? And that restaurant makes wonderful pie."

The big man scowled at her. "I don't want coffee or pie, and I'm tired of sitting around waiting on the rest of you."

Alice nearly volunteered to drive Max back to the hotel in Potterston when she recalled Jane's suggestion: *I think you should try to cheer him up, Alice. Treat him like one of your crankiest patients at the hospital.*

With an internal sigh, she abandoned her own shopping plans and decided to invite him to accompany her on her other task of the day. Perhaps away from the group he would feel more at ease and take some enjoyment in doing something different.

"I wonder, Max, since you have no shopping to do," Alice said, "if you would like to come with me to see our church."

His thick eyebrows drew together. "Why would I want to do that?"

"Grace Chapel is a wonderful little church." When his expression didn't change, she added, "I know it's not on the tour schedule, but it would give you something to do while the others are shopping and I would appreciate the company." *Please, God, don't let my nose grow longer.*

"Why are you going there?" he demanded. "Is there some sort of ladies' circle or prayer meeting going on? I'm not getting in the middle of that."

"No, I'm only picking up the flowers for the altar from the local florist and taking them over." She produced her best, guileless smile. "That's all."

"Is it?" Max stared at her for a long, silent moment.

What an unhappy, suspicious man. Suddenly she really wanted him to go with her. "It won't take very long," she prompted gently.

"I suppose I could. These people won't be happy until they've exhausted the limits on their credit cards," the businessman said finally.

"Thank you, Max."

Alice followed the minivan from Lloyd's house into town, and there parted company with the tour group. Max Ziglar's big, brooding presence at her side as she walked to the florist's was a bit unnerving, but she tried hard to act normal and chatted about Grace Chapel and her own youth ministry.

"You're a nurse, aren't you?" Max asked her.

"Yes, I work part-time at Potterston Hospital." She greeted the mother of one of her ANGELs in passing and then stopped at the corner of Hill Street and Acorn Avenue. "There is the florist's shop where I have to pick up the altar flower arrangements," she said, pointing across the street.

"'Wild Things,'" Max read from the shop's sign. "Does this woman specialize in wild flowers?"

Alice suppressed a giggle. "No, Craig Tracy—he's the florist—is something of a nonconformist."

"A *man* selling flowers?" Max's tone went chilly with disapproval. "I should say so."

Alice loved going into Wild Things, partly because Craig had the interior so artfully arranged with plants and flowers that it usually was a little like stepping into a rain forest. This time of year it was more like paying a visit to Santa's greenhouse. The shop glowed with poinsettias, holiday centerpieces, lovely decorated wreaths and tabletop Christmas trees.

She called Craig's name several times, but there was no answer.

"Craig sets up a small tent behind the shop every year to sell Christmas trees," Alice told Max. "He might be out there."

Max grunted. "He should get a bell."

"Alice!" Craig came from the back of the store to greet them. A slender man with short, light-brown hair that had a stubborn cowlick, he wore a dark green suit with a single red rosebud on his lapel. "I was wondering if you'd stop in today."

Alice introduced him to Max, who had been sizing up the younger man with a stern gaze.

"A pleasure to meet you, sir," Craig said, shaking his hand. "One of the women over at the Coffee Shop mentioned the Christmas homes tour. How do you like Acorn Hill?"

"It's different," was Max's terse response as he surveyed the interior of the shop.

"Things are a bit jumbled in here at the moment. I have a lot of orders being picked up," Craig said. "I also have to cover the Christmas tree lot out back." He turned to Alice. "You're here for the flowers for church, aren't you? I have them right over here."

Craig went to a temperature-controlled case that was stocked with several, delicate-looking floral arrangements.

"It's been so cold I've been keeping most of the flowers

in here." Carefully he extracted two large altar arrangements of white carnations, red roses and small pine branches studded with tiny brown cones. Each was simple but so well put together that it appeared perfectly balanced from every angle.

"Your flower arranger does fine work," Max said in a grudging way.

"I try," Craig said, and smiled as he covered the arrangements with some protective wrap and placed them in a shallow open box. "I fancy myself an artist. Flowers are my paint, and pots are my canvas. Of course, it would be a little easier if the palette wouldn't wilt on me."

Alice noticed Max's bleak expression deepening and hurried to thank Craig for his beautiful work. She was startled when Max turned down the florist's offer to bring the arrangements out to Alice's car and carried the box himself.

Why is he so short and disapproving toward younger men? She had noticed him treating Allan Hansford with a certain degree of civility, but he had been as terse and unfriendly with Craig as he had been with Ted Venson during the tour of Lloyd's home.

As she drove to Grace Chapel, Alice became aware that the big businessman had fallen into a brooding silence again and she decided to do something about it. "Do you have any family in the area, Max?"

"No." When she glanced sideways at him, he added, "I lost my wife ten years ago."

"I'm so sorry for your loss." She hesitated and then asked, "Did you have any children?"

"One son." He looked out through the passenger window. "John."

So Jane was wrong and he did have some family. "Will you be seeing him this Christmas?"

"No." Max gave her a sharp look. "Why are you asking me all these questions?"

"I'm just curious. I like meeting people and hearing about where they come from and what their families are like." She made a face. "I apologize if I'm being too nosy."

Max fell back into silence. Alice was trying to think of another topic of conversation when he suddenly spoke again. "My son and I don't speak to each other."

She wasn't sure how to respond to that. "Did you have an argument recently?"

"No. He defied me ten years ago and dropped out of business college. Said he wanted to be an *artist*." Max invested the last word with a great deal of contempt. "He went off to New York City and we haven't spoken since."

"I'm sorry to hear that." And she was.

"There's nothing to be sorry for. I have my business interests." He shifted his weight on the seat. "He's happy where he is, doing his pictures. He must make a little money at it. He's never asked me for any. Though God only knows how a man can make a reliable income with such work."

Alice felt terrible for pressing him on the subject, but that certainly explained his harsh attitude toward younger men, especially Ted and Craig, who were both very artistic. *They remind him of his son.*

"I'm not a parent, but I can imagine how difficult it has been for you."

"I don't know why I let it bother me. I suppose it's the holidays." He shook his head. "I can't even get in a decent week of work, what with the Christmas parties and everyone expecting time off. No use trying to keep the office open by myself."

"Is that why you took this tour?"

"I thought I'd get away from the city for a few days," he snapped. "Is that all right with you?"

There is always hope, Max, you just haven't found yours yet. She gave him a serene smile. "That's fine."

Chapter Eleven

*M*ax carried the floral arrangements into Grace Chapel for Alice and placed them on the altar tables.

"Nice little place," he said, looking around to admire the stained glass windows and simple arrangement of the polished oak pews.

The decorations committee had decided on shades of red, white and gold for the holidays this year, and Alice was proud to see how beautiful the church looked.

Red velvet bows with simple gold crosses against sprays of baby's breath adorned the window sills and the end of each pew. A Nativity scene with lifelike figures of Mary and Joseph and of the infant Jesus in a manger had been placed in a niche to the right of the altar, and a special spotlight illuminated the crèche.

The altar had not been neglected, either. Red and white poinsettias in brass pots formed a semicircle of bright color around the base of the altar rail. Over the center where the pastor gave his sermons, a large white star hung as a symbol of the season and a reminder of what first brought men to God's only Son.

"This place has the same name as your bed and breakfast place, doesn't it?" Max asked her.

"Yes. Our father was pastor here for over fifty years, so Grace Chapel has always been an important part of our lives. My sisters and I felt it was only natural to name our inn after it." Alice turned as a tall, dark-haired man emerged from a side door and approached them. "Here's our head pastor, Rev. Thompson."

"Good afternoon, Alice. I see you've picked up the flowers from Craig's." Rev. Thompson turned to Max and held out his hand. "Kenneth Thompson, welcome to Grace Chapel."

"Max Ziglar, how do you do?"

As the men shook hands, Alice could not help noticing the similarities between them. Both were tall and had something of a commanding presence. While Kenneth did not have as much bulk as the businessman, each had the kind of austere face that could make him seem unapproachable.

"Has Miss Howard brought your group to tour our church?" Kenneth's quiet smile transformed his features and made the kindness in his eyes much more noticeable.

Now if I could just get Max to do that, Alice thought. "The tour is wrapped up for the day and the others are shopping in town," she told the pastor. "Max was kind enough to help me with the flower arrangements."

"Miss Howard saved me from being dragged on yet another trek through the local shops," Max said more bluntly.

The reverend's eyes grew thoughtful as he studied the other man. "Are you a native of Boston, Max?"

"Born and raised, just outside Cambridge." He smiled. "You've got a good ear for accents. I thought after all these years down here, I'd gotten rid of mine."

"You have, very nearly. I'm predisposed to pick up a Boston accent," the pastor said. "My family is from Beacon Hill."

Alice rarely heard Rev. Thompson mention his childhood home, but Louise had told her that it was one of the most affluent areas in the city.

"Is that right?" Max Ziglar's attitude shifted and he regarded him with open curiosity now. "How does a rich boy from Beacon Hill end up a pastor in a small town in the middle of nowhere?"

"With the blessings of almighty God," Rev. Thompson said easily. "I know a number of people from the Cambridge area. Do you still have family there?"

"No. None at all." Max looked around as if searching for an avenue of escape. "Would you excuse me? I'm going to walk outside and get some air."

"Of course." With a heavy heart Alice watched the businessman trudge out of the church. When he had departed, she said, "I'm sorry, Pastor. Max is . . ." Like Louise, she was not sure what he was. Every time she thought she had him figured out, he did or said something to throw her off. There was one thing she was sure of, however. "Max is not a happy man."

"Why is he here with you instead of with his group?"

Alice related how Max had been disagreeable until she had coaxed him to come along with her to the church, and what he had told her about his wife and son on the drive over.

"I know he's only here for one more day," she told the reverend, "but I'd like to do something to help him feel a little of the Christmas spirit, if I can."

"Spending the holidays alone after years of sharing them with a wife and family can be painful," the pastor said gently. "As you know, my wife and I didn't have children, but after her death I felt her loss most keenly during the holidays. Being around others who still have their families with them is particularly difficult. You can't help but envy them."

She had never thought of the problem from that perspective. At the same time, she understood missing a loved one. Christmas was not the same without her father. "How did you deal with it, Pastor?"

"I can never replace Catherine, but after her death my ministry gave my life renewed purpose and direction. In a sense, I allowed my congregations here and in Boston to become my extended family." His gaze went to the Nativity scene. "It is at Christmas that I always think of the passage from Psalm 138:3 [KJV]: 'In the day when I cried thou answeredst me, and strengthenedst me with strength in my soul.'"

"I don't think that I can convince Max Ziglar to take up a life of service in one day." She made a face. "I can't even get him to go into shops."

"He feels like an outsider, Alice. It's also a matter of what he's comfortable with. That's probably why he works so hard to keep people from getting close to him."

That made sense to her. "I wish I could have brought him to my last ANGELs meeting. The girls are always so cheerful and full of energy, and they wouldn't remind him of his son."

Rev. Thompson looked up as the door to the church opened and Max came back inside. "You know, I think I may be able to help."

After Max had rejoined them, the reverend surprised Alice when he invited the businessman to have dinner with him at the rectory.

"I haven't had the opportunity to talk about Boston

with anyone in a long time," he said, when Max began to refuse. "Did you follow the Red Sox this year?"

"I'm a Bostonian, I have no choice," Max grumbled. "I still cannot believe what happened during the playoffs. Did you catch game three with the Yankees?"

"Unhappily, I did."

As the men chatted about baseball, Alice felt a little glimmer of hope. *Maybe the pastor is right, maybe this will work.*

$\backsim$

Alice related Max Ziglar's sad story to Louise and Jane later that night at the inn, and immediately her two sisters saw the businessman in a different light.

"I wouldn't feel very cheerful listening to everyone chatter on about their families while all I had to look forward to was going home to an empty house," Alice said. She gave her sisters a sorrowful look. "Which is where I would be right now, if you two hadn't come back home."

As a widow, Louise understood how difficult it was to maintain a positive outlook after the loss of a spouse, and the thought of being estranged from her daughter Cynthia was abhorrent, so she could sympathize with Max's bitterness over his son.

The only aspect that still troubled her was that Max Ziglar remained estranged from his son ten years after the

death of his wife. Surely by now he might have found a way
to mend the breach between them.

"You left him with Pastor Thompson?" she asked Alice.

"Kenneth insisted and Max had no objections. They
were still talking about runs batted in or something when I
left the church." Her short brown hair bobbed as she shook
her head. "I will never understand what men find so fascinating about sports statistics."

"It's inherent in the male of the species," Louise said.
She looked over at Jane, who had been particularly quiet.
"You will have to handle Laura and Max tomorrow evening
when you go to tour the Bellwoods' home. Are you up to
the task, my dear?"

"I can swing it, I think." Jane rested her chin against
one hand. "What was Max's son's name again, Alice?"

"John. Why?"

"I was just curious. You said he was an artist. I was hoping someone might have heard of him." Jane shrugged and
added, "Do you need anything for the hospital party?"

"No, I have everything packed up and ready to go."
Alice brought out the boxes of handmade stockings that
her ANGELs had filled with small, donated gifts for the
children's ward patients at Potterston Hospital. "I checked
with the ward nurse, and we have more than enough stockings for the current inpatients and anyone who might be

admitted over the next few days. All we have to do is meet Lloyd and Pastor Thompson in the lobby after dinner."

"Lloyd's going with you?" Jane asked.

"Pastor Thompson convinced the mayor to hand out the stockings to the children," Louise told her. "I would imagine that Lloyd will make a very convincing Santa Claus."

The next morning, however, disaster struck when Lloyd telephoned the inn to tell Louise and Alice that he would not be able to accompany them to the hospital.

"I woke up this morning with a fever," he said, his voice very hoarse, "and it feels like I'm getting the flu." He paused to sneeze and then apologized. "I don't want to risk infecting any of the children."

"Go to bed and rest," Louise told him. "I am sure we can find someone else to play Santa."

Unfortunately, every likely candidate the Howard sisters called had prior commitments and as a result was unable to take the mayor's place. In mid-afternoon Louise telephoned the pastor to pass along the bad news. Kenneth Thompson didn't seem worried, and since he had the Santa Claus costume with him, he took responsibility for finding a last-minute replacement.

"I think I know the perfect person for the job," he told her. "I will meet you and Alice at the children's ward at seven, as we planned."

After dinner, Jane had to leave to escort the tour to the Bellwoods' home and her sisters had to get ready for their party. Louise took care to dress in her brightest holiday outfit, a long-sleeved, dark-blue dress with large silver stars and snowflakes decorating the fabric. She came downstairs to find her middle sister carrying the boxes of stockings from the kitchen.

Alice, who was playing the part of Santa's helper, had dressed in a dark-red sweater, brown corduroy slacks and Aunt Ethel's jaunty, green knit hat with the white pompom to complete her outfit.

"You look positively elfin," Louise told her.

Alice grinned. "While you look like the Queen of Winter." She set the boxes by the front door and thought for a moment. "We have the stockings ready, some of my ANGELs are coming by to help pass them out and the pastor will be there to officiate. All we need is Santa to make his appearance."

"I'm still curious about whom the minister will draft to play Lloyd's role," Louise said as she slipped on her gloves and coat. "Do you think he asked Henry Ley to fill in?"

"No, Henry and Patsy are out of town. Patsy told me that they were spending the holiday with relatives in Maryland." Alice followed her out to the car, but hesitated and looked toward the trees at the edge of the property.

The full moon had come out and illuminated the landscape with soft, silvery light. "That's odd."

"What is, dear?" Louise followed her gaze.

"Jane and I hung up all those pinecone bird feeders yesterday, and there were birds in every tree." She nodded toward the peanut butter and birdseed encrusted cones. "We resupplied them today, but apparently there have been no birds around to feed at them. It's just like Fred said."

Louise rubbed her gloves against her ears. "They have probably been off snuggling in a hollow trunk, if they have any sense. It is freezing out here."

"I guess you're right." Her middle sister gave their homemade bird feeders one more worried glance. "I hope they come back."

Alice drove to the hospital in Potterston, where they found the ANGELs waiting for them in the lobby. Five girls from Alice's preteen ministry group were dressed in their holiday best. They appeared eager to hand out the stockings their group had made over the autumn for the young patients at the hospital.

"You look terrific, Mrs. Smith," Sissy Matthews, Louise's most dedicated piano student, said. "Do you think the kids will like what we made for them, Miss Howard?"

The project had actually been Sissy's idea, after Alice told the group about the sick and injured children on the pediatric ward who would not be able to spend Christmas at home with their families.

"I think they will love it, honey." She surveyed the other girls with a smile. "Has anyone seen Pastor Thompson and Santa yet?"

"They went upstairs to see the kids a little while ago," another girl confirmed. "That Santa Claus wasn't Mayor Tynan, though, Miss Howard."

"But he was awfully big." Sissy giggled. "His trousers weren't long enough to cover his ankles."

In fact, none of the girls knew who had come to the hospital to play Santa, which seemed somewhat strange to Louise. But then she, Alice and the girls went up to the ward and saw Rev. Thompson and Santa visiting with the ambulatory kids in the patient playroom.

"Is it true that you bring presents down the chimney on Christmas Eve?" one little boy with bandages on his neck and shoulder asked as he climbed onto Santa's knee.

"I do indeed." A big hand in a white glove steadied the little patient.

His answer made the child's expression turn woebegone. "But we don't have any chimneys here at the hospital."

"I will tell you a secret," Santa said, making his deep voice drop to a theatrical whisper. "When there are no chimneys, I use doors."

A second boy hobbled over on crutches. "Can you make my leg straight, Santa?"

Santa's dark eyes went to the complicated-looking orthopedic boot encasing the child's foot and calf.

One of the nurses stepped forward. "Your doctor will do everything he can to help your leg heal, Peter."

The boy's lower lip wobbled. "But can't Santa do that with magic now, so I can go home?"

"I'm not a doctor, son," Santa said honestly. "No magic can replace the time your leg needs to heal, either."

"At least you only have one hurt leg," a little girl in a wheelchair said. She had heavy casts on both of her legs.

"If there was something else you could have for Christmas," Santa asked the boy on crutches, "what would it be?"

"A new baseball glove," the boy said promptly. "I play shortstop, and my old one is getting too small."

"Alice," Louise said in a low voice, "is that ...?"

Her sister stared through the playroom window. "I think it is." She blinked deliberately. "How did Kenneth manage this?"

Louise only shook her head, still dumbfounded.

Alice led her ANGELs, letting the girls be the ones to pass out the gift stockings to the young patients. Louise went to stand beside Pastor Thompson and watched as

Santa crouched down beside the girl in the wheelchair to ask what she wanted him to bring to her on Christmas Day.

"Something to scratch my itches," the little girl said, and thumped a small fist against one of the plaster casts. "I can't get at them with these on."

A slight smile appeared under the white mustache and beard that Santa wore. "Santa can show you how to do that right now, sweetheart." He rose and after a brief consultation with one of the attending nurses, went over to a shelf where various games were kept for the children.

"Pastor, I'm speechless," Louise murmured. "How on earth did you bring this about?"

"It only took a little persuasion." He smiled down at her. "I believe that he needed something exactly like this to happen."

Santa returned with a thin, blunt-tipped stick about the length of a drinking straw.

Alice came over to join them. "I'm amazed, Pastor. Maybe you can also help me find a gift to give to Jane for Christmas."

"Remember, it's not the gift that is important, Alice," he told her, "as much as the love with which it is given."

By that time Santa had showed the little girl how to insert the thin blunt-tipped plastic stick under the edge of her cast.

"You should always ask a nurse or grownup to help you do this, or you might scratch the skin inside," he told her as he showed her how to funnel the stick into her cast. "But if you're careful, it will scratch all your itchy spots under there."

"Thank you, Santa!" the little girl threw her arms around Max's neck and gave him a grateful hug.

Chapter Twelve

*J*ane was looking forward to doing her part as guide for the tour group. Since it was the group's last day in Acorn Hill, she planned to make it a memorable one. She was also firmly committed to avoiding busywork for the rest of her vacation.

After this I will go home and spend time with my sisters, and stop being such a ninny about the holidays.

As she waited in town for the tour group late that afternoon, she took a moment to walk by the Good Apple Bakery. Clarissa Cottrell was decorating gingerbread men on a table at the front of the store. Three small children, two girls and one boy, stood pressing their noses against the glass panes and watching. The children wore matching white and green striped knit caps with red pompoms on the crowns.

Jane joined the wide-eyed youngsters and smiled at their mother, who was resting on a bench in front of the bakery. "Wow, those look terrific, don't they?"

"She's making the eyes and buttons out of raisins," one of the little girls told her solemnly. "Mommy says that's because raisins taste better in gingerbread and they don't melt like chocolate chips."

"Look!" the boy tapped the window. "She's putting on hats like ours."

The smiling Clarissa piped white, green and red icing on three of the large cookies before holding them up for the children to see.

"Be right back." Jane went inside the warm, fragrant bakery and returned a minute later bearing three gingerbread men, which she presented to the children. "You have to save these for after dinner," she warned, "or your mom will get mad at me."

Jane saw the tour minivan pull up by Town Hall, so she excused herself to meet the group. There were only four of them, and Edwina explained that Max had opted for not taking part.

"I think he made other plans," she said, looking a little puzzled. "To do what, I can't say, but he was quite adamant."

"Oh well." Jane shrugged. "We'll simply have to have a fabulous time and make him sorry he missed it."

The rest of the group didn't appear very enthusiastic. Edwina looked tired; Allan had red, watery eyes and kept sneezing into a handkerchief; Ted seemed nervous and fiddled with his camera; and Laura kept tapping her foot as if everyone else were keeping her from an important appointment.

Maybe it's a good thing that I don't have to deal with Max Ziglar, Jane thought. "We are going to have a great time tonight, I promise. Samuel and Rose's farm is one of the nicest in the area, and their house is simply fantastic. Just follow me."

On the way to the Bellwoods' home, Jane noticed in her mirror that the van seemed to be having some mechanical trouble. The engine stalled twice on the driver when he stopped at intersections, and she thought that the amount of white exhaust coming from his tailpipe seemed rather excessive.

When they reached their destination just outside of town, Jane got out of her car, went up to the minivan and tapped on the driver's window.

"Are you having some trouble?" She pointed to the engine.

The driver rolled down the window as his passengers left the vehicle. "I am, miss. I'm going to head over to the garage in Potterston while you folks are here and have the mechanic take a look at it—they're open until nine. If necessary, I'll see if I can arrange for another van while I'm there."

"Is there some way I can get in touch with you?"

He wrote something on a piece of notepaper and handed it to her. "Call me at this number when they're ready to go."

"Is everything all right?" Edwina asked when Jane rejoined the group. "The van was acting up on the drive over."

Jane nodded. "Your driver is going to have it looked at. As soon as he takes care of things, he'll be back." She knew Rose Bellwood would not mind if they stayed here a bit longer after the tour.

Samuel and Rose Bellwood lived on one of the small, family-owned farm properties near Acorn Hill. Jane was glad it was the last stop on the Christmas homes tour because it was one of her favorite places to visit for the holidays.

"Our friends the Bellwoods both come from farming backgrounds," Jane told the group as they walked up the pretty cobblestone path to the front door of the two-story, white farmhouse. "Samuel was raised in Idaho on his family's potato farm, and Rose's father ran a stock auction business in Lancaster County, which is the heart of Amish country. They met in college, and when they married, Sam's father gave them this land as a wedding gift, and Rose's father gave them enough sheep to start their first flock."

"Do the Bellwoods still raise sheep?" Edwina asked.

Jane nodded. "They certainly do. Samuel and Rose raise Merino sheep, which produce some of the finest quality wool in the world. They also grow most of their own feed." She concentrated for a moment to recall the tour literature she had studied the previous night. "The architectural style of this farmhouse is considered folk Victorian, with some modifications. Samuel and Rose have made extensive improvements to the original house, which was built just before 1900."

The long, white house looked very warm and inviting. It was the quintessential farm home, big and sprawling, with solid lines and delightful details, like the round, green-and-red hex sign above the main entry door, which had been painted with an intricate folk art design of tulips and hearts around two birds, a star and the German word *wilkum*.

"Our region of Pennsylvania is famous for hex signs," Jane said as she pointed it out. "You'll see them painted on the sides of barns and over the doors of homes. Although the word *hex* suggests otherwise, these folk art signs are not symbols of superstition. The first German settlers used them to decorate many things, from furniture to pottery to birth certificates. And, to dispel a popular myth, the Amish don't paint hex signs on their homes or barns."

"I understand that *wilkum* means welcome," Edwina said, "but what does the rest of the design mean, Jane?"

"The birds are distelfinks, which are believed to bring good fortune and happiness. The star has long been regarded to be a symbol of luck and bounty."

Jane was glad for the glimmer of moonlight. Along with the exterior lights, it allowed her to show the group what Samuel and his wife had done to the farmhouse over the years to accommodate their needs.

"Folk Victorian houses usually have a square look to them, which Samuel altered when he built the east and west extensions, as well as the extra rooms on the attic level." She pointed out each addition. "Under the eaves you can see the scrolled brackets that are typical of folk Victorian style. The brackets, along with a lot of the decorative trim for the house, were actually mass-produced at the end of the nineteenth century and shipped via railroad out West."

"Why did they do that, Jane?" Ted Venson asked as he took a photo of a particularly intricate bracket piece.

The flash from his camera made spots appear in front of her eyes for a moment. "I don't know, to be honest. That's just what the literature your tour company sent me said." Jane eyed Allan Hansford. "But I'll wager our friendly architect here can help me out."

"Settlers of the period often didn't have access to skilled carpenters or sophisticated woodworking machinery," he said, his voice a bit hoarse. "Pieces could be ordered individually or by lot, which allowed the home builders in thinly settled areas to design their homes according to their personal preferences." He pulled out his handkerchief again to catch a sneeze. "I beg your pardon."

"God bless you," Jane said, feeling a little concerned. "Mr. Hansford, if you're not feeling well, I'd be happy to try contacting your driver so he can take you back to your hotel."

If the van would make it that far.

"It's only my allergies, Ms. Howard. I took a tablet this evening after dinner and that should start clearing up the symptoms soon." He smiled up at the house. "I don't want to miss the tour of this home. I haven't had many opportunities to see a working farm, and the house itself has some remarkable attributes. You see the spindle work all along the porch here?" He pointed to the white-painted wood turnings. "This was done by hand, not machine. You can tell from the slight irregularities in the notching. All of the trim appears to be original, which says something about the owner for taking the trouble to preserve it."

Jane thanked him for the information and finished the presentation on the exterior by pointing out the low pitch of the pyramid roof, the typical front gable and the absence of the usual side wings. "Because the original owner was a widower who never remarried, he built the house as a bachelor's residence. Samuel and Rose added new rooms as their children came along, so the house grew with their family, as did the amount of livestock they raised."

Jane's breath came out in white puffs in the air as she told the group about the barns and shearing sheds on the property. Her nose had gone completely numb by the time she finished.

"There is more I'm supposed to tell you, according to the literature, but we'd all be Popsicles by the time I did," she said, earning a grateful look from Ted, who was shivering so much that he stopped taking photos. "So I vote we go inside and meet the Bellwoods."

"Seconded," Edwina said.

As Jane led the group into the glass-enclosed front entryway, she didn't have to tell them that Samuel had installed an area heater for the porch. The transition from the frigid temperature outside to the comfortable warmth made everyone break into immediate sighs of relief.

"The Bellwoods have hosted a living crèche here at the farm every Christmas Eve since I can remember," she said as she walked up to ring the doorbell. "When my sisters and I were girls, coming to welcome the birth of baby Jesus was one of the highlights of our Christmas vacation."

Rose Bellwood answered the door and greeted Jane. Samuel's wife, a petite brunette with a gentle smile, wore her long, dark-brown hair in a crown of braids. She gestured for the group to come in. "You all look so cold. Come into the kitchen. I have some tea and hot apple cider prepared."

The front foyer branched off in three directions, opening up to a wide stairwell to the right, a living room to the center and the kitchen to the left.

Because four of their five grown children had settled in the area, and their youngest, who was attending Penn State, often brought friends home, Samuel had knocked out a wall to transform their utility room into an oversize dining area.

"We always had most of our family meals in the kitchen

when the children were growing up," Rose told them. Her merry brown eyes sparkled as she surveyed her kitchen. "Now I have a perfectly beautiful, formal dining room, but the family still prefers eating in here." She lowered her voice to a confidential tone. "To be honest, so do I."

If there was one kitchen Jane loved almost as much as Grace Chapel Inn's, it was Rose Bellwood's. Cabinets of blonde burl oak with glass fronts were set above wide, dark green marble-topped counters. The appliances were all new, sleek and in the same dark-cream shade as the cabinet wood.

The amount of natural light was another thing that Jane loved. Samuel had installed two additional windows on either side of the sink window, which permitted sunlight to illuminate the entire room. Little brass pots, in which Rose grew herbs during the summer, lined the windowsills.

A four-foot-tall bar in the same oak and marble formed a half-divider between the kitchen and dining area, providing a spot for a quick sandwich or snack. The dining area was as large as the kitchen and contained a sturdy, rustic-looking farmhouse table covered with a red-and-white-checked cloth. Six spindle-back chairs padded with matching cushions accompanied the table.

Rose had the promised cider and tea waiting, as well as a platter of corn muffins and sugar-dusted fruit turnovers.

"Oh, Rose, you shouldn't have gone to all this trouble," Jane chastised her.

"Nonsense, it's like the arctic outside. You folks sit down for a spell." She guided them toward the chairs. "The house isn't going anywhere."

Jane could not have asked for a better beginning. The group sat around the table warming themselves with the hot drinks and enjoying the baked goods, while Rose answered their questions about the history on the house.

"The farm was originally planned as a dairy, and in its heyday it provided most of the milk, cheese and butter for the people living in Acorn Hill." Rose nodded toward the town. "Once refrigeration made it possible to ship and store perishables, however, the dairy began slowly losing business. When Samuel and I took it over from the retired owner, we decided to try our hand at raising wool sheep."

Rose got up for a moment to fetch an envelope from the counter. From it she extracted some old, black-and-white photographs. "This is what the house looked like originally, before Sam and I took over."

"Buying a farm must have seemed risky, though," Allan commented. "I assume neither of you had experience raising sheep."

"I knew a lot about animals from working with my father, and Samuel had raised just about every type of critter you can think of on his family's farm in Idaho. Still, when he told me that he thought we should become shepherds only a week after we were married . . ." She chuckled softly and pressed a hand to her cheek. "Let's just say it required a real leap of faith for me."

Because both Samuel and Rose were very close to Rose's parents and siblings, all of whom resided in the area, they had plenty of help with the initial work to convert the old dairy into a sheep farm.

"We certainly needed it too," she told them. "We were fortunate in that the house and the property had been properly maintained over the years, but it was quite a job modifying the barn and livestock sheds. I had a little Kodak camera my folks had given me when I graduated from high school and I used that to take pictures as Samuel and my brothers converted the milking parlor for shearing sheep."

Rose passed the photographs around the table.

The first ones showed the original condition of the large shed where the cows had been milked, along with younger versions of the Bellwoods. "Is there a big difference between raising sheep and cows, Rose?" Jane asked.

"Sheep are a little better at herding and grazing than cattle. They'll actually control some of the forage problems in a pasture by eating the weeds. Unfortunately, they're also more time-intensive, and because of their size, they can be more vulnerable to injury and certain predators." She sighed. "Then there was our first lambing season. My poor Samuel spent weeks in the lambing jugs—those are special, temporary pens—shearing the mothers before they gave birth. Then the little ones started coming, and I thought at one point the entire flock would lamb overnight." She shook her head, remembering. "We were truly fortunate to have the good Lord's blessings and the help of my family that first spring."

Jane sorted through the photos, which showed the gradual transformation of the farm. In one shot Samuel and Rose's brothers were digging out a large, oval hole in the ground. "I didn't know you had a pool, Rose."

"Never did. That became our shearing pond. The sheep have to be washed before they're sheared," Rose said. "It's much easier to clean the wool while it is still on the animal than it is to wash fleeces, so the children and I would do that while Samuel and my brothers sheared." A fond smile curved her mouth. "Chasing the sheep into the pond was always great fun for us, but I suspect the kids liked getting wet much more than our sheep did."

"Do you still work with your husband tending to the animals, Mrs. Bellwood?" Ted asked.

"Yes. Our farm has always been a partnership effort, and why should I let him have all the fun?" Her eyes twinkled. "My husband also claims that there isn't a man in the county who can shear a sheep faster than I can."

Chapter Thirteen

*W*hen they had finished their snack, Rose took them back to the living room to begin the tour.

Four slender columns of pale-gray ash supported matching ceiling beams, from which a small galaxy of unusually shaped, golden, paper stars hung. Reproduction Shaker and Amish furniture drew the eye with their clean lines and jewel-toned upholstery, and were complemented by the dark green Christmas tree the Bellwoods had decorated with gilded nuts, flowers and myriad colorful ornaments, many of them obviously made by their children at an early age and carefully treasured ever since.

What most commanded attention were the six quilts Rose had displayed on the walls like fine tapestries. Jane loved the Amish and Mennonite quilts, which were all variations of the classic sunshine-and-shadow patchwork pattern, pairing bright primary color fabrics with rich dark greens, browns and blacks.

"This is where we mostly congregate when we're not out in the barn or in the kitchen," Rose said. "I do my needlework there"—she pointed toward a comfortable armchair beside which stood an oval quilt frame—"and Samuel uses that old desk in the corner there to work on accounts in the evening."

"A farmer never runs out of weeds or paperwork," Samuel Bellwood said as he joined them. The farmer was a tall, solid man who seemed to dwarf everything around him. Years of working outdoors had tanned his skin, against which his kind blue eyes seemed clear and bright. He smiled at his wife. "Hello, all."

The group returned his greeting.

Rose went to hug her gentle giant of a husband. "I thought you'd be too busy in the barn to come in."

"The stock decided they'd rather be warm and dry than make a fuss," he said, "so I finished up early." He checked his watch. "Vera Humbert called a little while ago and said she'd be dropping by with some quilts for your next guild display over at Town Hall."

"Keep an ear out for her while I take these folks upstairs, would you, dear?" Rose asked her husband.

Jane and Rose accompanied the group to the second floor, which featured five spacious bedrooms and a library that Rose said had been a study room for her children when they were young.

"We've always emphasized the importance of study and

homework," Rose told Edwina as she brought them into the library. "But with running the farm and caring for the family it wasn't easy for me to keep track of their progress. It always seemed like one of them wanted to do homework at the precise time that the other wanted to have a friend over to play. We had the room, so I thought, why not turn it into our own little classroom?"

"Wouldn't you have rather have made this into something for yourself?" Laura seemed rather mystified by the concept.

"Oh, I've slipped in there myself a few times, for a peaceful hour of reading or writing letters." Rose smiled. "Now we keep it for our grandchildren when they stay over, so you could call it a real 'family room.'"

Samuel joined them to let Rose know that Vera had arrived, and offered to take the group out to the barn where the Bellwoods held their living crèche every year. Before they left the house, Samuel retrieved the group's coats and outerwear, which Rose had hung on pegs near the fireplace to warm. The family's dog, a bright-eyed, black-and-white Sheltie named Missy, went with them.

The walk out to the main barn was short but very cold. Inside the large, red-painted building, two rows of straw-filled stalls were home to the farm's four stock horses and three milk cows. The cows were placidly chewing their cud and only eyed the group through the wood stall slats, but the big, soft-eyed horses stretched their heads out to have a look and whinny a welcome.

Missy went up to each stall as if greeting the horses, then barked at one of the barn cats, who beat a hasty retreat.

"Our dog would run this entire farm, if I let her," Samuel confided to the group. "Shelties are wonderful herding dogs, but she tends to herd everything—even me and Rose."

"How does one herd sheep in these modern times?" Allan asked.

"My modern-thinking sons like using their all-terrain vehicles, but I've always preferred riding a horse," Samuel said after he introduced each of the animals by name. "An ATV can't sense things the way a horse can." Samuel chuckled as one of the horses nickered and bumped the farmer's shoulder with his head. "Or have as big a hankering for sweets." He fished some sugar cubes from his jacket pocket and gave each of the horses a treat.

A young heifer and two small lambs had been placed in a special, open-front area at the far end of the barn, where Samuel brought the group next.

"Rose and I started to do this when our kids were small, because we wanted them to understand the story of baby Jesus from the Bible," he told the group. "It is one thing to read about the Nativity, but quite another to see and feel and hear what it must have been like for the Holy Family."

One of Samuel's sons arrived with his two boys. Each brought a shepherd's costume sewn by his mother for the reenactment. After introducing them to the group, Samuel took the boys down to the special stall the Bellwoods reserved for the living Nativity.

Inside the stall, Samuel had constructed a reproduction of the classic manger scene using real elements from his barn—such as grain bins, water troughs and bales of straw. The centerpiece was a very small, plain hay manger, which held a soft blue baby blanket draped over a fluffy mound of very fine dried grass.

Jane couldn't help sighing as she looked at the soft, wondering eyes of the baby animals. "We never needed a petting zoo in Acorn Hill," she told the group. "We would just come over to the Bellwoods'."

"Where I would put them to work," the farmer joked. "Jane here is very handy with a pitchfork."

Samuel explained how at first only the Bellwood children acted out the parts in their living crèche. "They wanted to show their friends, of course, so we allowed them to invite over some kids from school for the reenactment. Those children wanted to join in the fun, and as you know you can never have too many angels or shepherds. Then they went home and told their folks about it, and before long we had a couple dozen families from church involved in the project every year." He looked at his grandsons, who had climbed into the stall and were petting the two baby lambs. "This year one of my ewes decided to drop a pair of twins early, so we decided to have them be a part of the crèche."

"You don't have any Christmas lights strung in here," Laura commented. "Don't you think it would look more festive if you added something like a lighted star?"

"We try to keep it exactly as it was two thousand years ago," Samuel told her. "The lights we save for the house and our tree."

"I think it's marvelous that you do this for the community," Edwina said as she reached over to pet one of the lambs who had wandered over to the low gate. Missy came to stand and watch the boys with her bright, dark eyes. "How many people come to see the reenactment now?"

"Several hundred, so we've started doing repeat performances spread out over Christmas week," the farmer said. "We also play host to a number of Christian groups who want to celebrate the real reason for the season. This year we'll be hosting a choir from Wilkes-Barre who will be filming their performance here for a local cable television station."

"Your fifteen minutes of fame," Jane teased.

"Rose thought I should wear a suit." Samuel grinned as he held up the robes his daughter-in-law had sewn. "But lucky for me, the poor shepherds keeping watch over their flocks weren't able to afford double-breasted jackets."

The temperature had dropped so quickly that by the time Samuel, Jane and the group had returned to the farmhouse they were all thoroughly chilled. Rose escorted everyone to the living room for a last, warming cup of spiced cider before the long ride back to the hotel in Potterston. She introduced the group to Vera Humbert, who had stayed to say hello to Jane.

"These folks are certainly the nicest group we've had this year," Rose said to Jane apart from the others and glanced at Allan. "That gentleman there knows so much about old houses. I'll wager he would make a wonderful teacher."

"I've already learned so much listening to him that my head hurts," Jane admitted with a laugh.

When Allan asked if he could get a glass of water from the kitchen in order to take some of his allergy tablets, Jane decided to go with him.

She passed along the compliment Rose had given him, and then asked, "What made you decide to retire, Allan?"

"I saved a little every week when I was working so that

I could retire early," Allan said as he took out his pills. "All of our friends were doing it, selling their houses and moving to places like Florida to live on golf courses and spend their golden years in the sun."

She got him a glass of water from the sink. "But you're still living here in Pennsylvania."

"My wife and I aren't much for golf." He paused to swallow the tablets and chase them down with the water. "I haven't done much but putter around the house since I left the firm, but I intend to write a book about architecture someday."

"Why don't you write one now?"

"I have this problem. Every time I sit down to do it, my mind goes completely blank and stays that way." He chuckled. "I was always better at sketching and making presentation models than I was at writing."

"Have you ever thought about teaching?"

He emptied the glass in the sink. "Mrs. Bellwood was very kind to say that about me, but I don't see myself as the type who would make a very good instructor."

"That's not what I hear from my sisters, and tonight you taught us a lot about this house."

"Oh, that was nothing." He made an offhand gesture. "I just like talking about architecture."

"But that's what teaching is," she said, "getting a bunch of youngsters together and talking with them about what you know. I suspect it would be a lot more fun for you than puttering around the house."

He seemed taken aback by that. "Maybe it would be."

When Jane and Allan returned to the group, they found Rose answering questions about her unique decorations.

"I can't recall ever seeing flowers on a Christmas tree or stars like these, Mrs. Bellwood," Ted said, nodding toward the paper stars hanging from the beams. "Are they European?"

"Those are Moravian stars, which are traditional Pennsylvania Dutch decorations." Rose picked up a small, plain-looking wooden box from a collection of them on a side table and opened it. A tiny mechanism inside whirred into life and played the opening bars of "Away in a Manger." "And these are my caroling music boxes. Neither Samuel nor I are musically talented, so when the children were little, we would wind these up and play the tunes while they sang the songs."

"My family could have used some of those when I was a kid," Jane said. She was tone-deaf and as a result could not sing on key, something that confounded her more musical sisters. "They might have drowned me out."

"These flowers on your tree are real," Laura Lattimer said as she tested the petal of a rose.

"So are the nuts." Rose exchanged an amused glance with Jane before she added, "That's another tradition in this part of the country. The Amish started it, I believe, because they don't hold with commercialism of any kind, especially of the holidays. Their Christmas trees are usually decorated only with fruit, nuts and live flowers."

Vera asked Rose if she had shown the group some of her antique Amish quilts. "Rose started collecting quilts the same time I did," she told Jane. "It's how we became friends."

"We very nearly didn't," the farmer's wife said. "At first, all we did was try to outbid each other at auctions."

Vera and Rose took the group through the rest of the rooms on the first floor, each of which had at least two quilts on display. Some hung like tapestries, others were folded neatly on standing racks. All were made in traditional patchwork patterns.

"Most of my quilts are at least one hundred years old," Rose told the group. "Old quilts can't take much direct exposure to sunlight, so to keep them from fading, I rotate them every other month with others I have safely stored."

"Vera is quite a quilt historian," Jane told the group. Earlier in the fall, Fred's wife had saved an old quilt she and her sisters had inadvertently thrown out, and had given them a great deal of information about its significance.

"After Fred and the girls, they are my passion," she admitted.

"We try to get her to speak at all the big guild meetings," Rose said. "I know I've learned more from her than from any book I've ever read."

"Well, I'm going to take advantage of that," Edwina said. "When did people start making quilts, Vera?"

"Quilt-making dates back to ancient Egypt, and knights used to wear quilted padding under their armor to protect their skin, but quilts in America are only about three hundred years old."

Rose told them of the trip that she, Vera and her quilting guild had made to the Smithsonian the year before, to see quilts made as far back as 1780. "I thought the curator would never let us out of there once Vera identified a quilt for which they had been trying to find a pattern name."

"What made quilts so popular here in America?" Laura asked. "They're only bed covers."

"The first American colonists had a very hard time of it," Vera told the younger woman. "Fabric, thread and needles were expensive because they had to be brought over from England. Most households produced their own woolen homespun, as cotton wouldn't become available until after the invention of the cotton gin in 1793. Mostly the women of the time made their clothes from imported fabrics like linen and silks, or their own woven wool. They made their quilts from the same materials."

"I thought the women of that period made their quilts from worn clothing," Edwina said.

"Scrap quilts made of clothing came much later, during the Civil War, when blockades and fighting kept disrupting supply lines," Vera said. "Until the war most women chose to weave blankets rather than make quilts. During the war, even homespun was needed for clothing and any scraps were considered too dear to waste."

Vera helped Rose take out some of her quilts to show them different styles and techniques. "When quilting became more popular in the nineteenth century, it became a skill young women were expected to learn. You can see from this Ohio Star quilt"—she unfolded a large, blue-and-red quilt with patchwork that formed eight-pointed stars—"how the quilting was in straight lines, or what we call 'in the ditch.'"

Vera shared her knowledge about the period after the Civil War, when the sewing machine made its impact upon quilting. Women began making scrap quilts from the silk dresses they had once worn.

"The first sewing machine was designed as a cobbler's tool, to make shoes," she told the group. "Isaac Singer designed a sewing machine with a foot treadle that allowed the sewer to keep her hands free to move the fabric under the needle. He made the machine affordable, too, so that nearly every woman in America could have one in her home. Since machine sewing was a hundred times faster than hand sewing, quilt making became far easier and more popular."

"What sort of quilts were made after the war, Mrs. Humbert?" Edwina asked.

"Wool quilts were always a favorite, because people needed to keep warm. But the sewing machine allowed women to sew more for pleasure, and they began making what we call art quilts. Redwork, or white quilts with embroidered pictures in red thread, were all the rage at one point, and so too were crazy quilts, which were randomly pieced fancy fabrics with embroidery on the seams and patches. Quilters began embellishing their patchwork with all kinds of beads, fancy stitching and flowers made of silk ribbon or cut tuft work. Some quilters even painted little pictures on their quilts."

"I've always liked the quilts from the thirties," Rose said as she took out two examples from that era, a classic double wedding ring, and a tumbling blocks quilt to show them the improvement in fabric dyes. "This is when women were able to get more pastel and candy-colored fabrics. Dyes stopped running and fading, and prints became more elaborate."

"Your quilts were made by Amish or Mennonite quilt makers, weren't they, Rose?" Jane asked.

"Mostly, yes, although I do have a few Amish-style quilts now that I've made myself or with my quilting guild. Hand quilting takes time and patience," she explained, "and

Amish quilt patterns may look simple, but they're very demanding pieces to make."

Rose told them how in the late seventeenth century a Swiss farmer named Joseph Amman had convinced many Mennonites to leave their church and form the founding families of the Amish religion.

"Bishop Amman wanted to preserve their heritage and follow the religious ideal of living a plain, simple life as they interpreted it from the Bible. Soon after the Amish split, they came to America and settled first in Lancaster County, then all over this region of Pennsylvania."

Rose explained how quilting became both an art form and a method of socialization for Amish women. "Their quilts were always made entirely by hand. Although the quilts are almost always in solid colors and very basic patchwork designs, the designs themselves were never affected by the outside world. There are women in Amish country today who are making quilts from the same templates that their great-great-grandmothers used."

"Completely untouched by time," Ted said, snapping several photos.

"Even when Isaac Singer threw himself into marketing the first treadle sewing machine to every woman in America, very few Amish women actually bought them," Rose said.

Edwina frowned. "But I thought it saved them so much time."

Vera grinned. "A sewing machine is a modern contraption —the use of which is forbidden by their religious beliefs— but to tell you the truth, I think Amish women knew their quilts were spectacular because of the hand stitching."

Jane was surprised to hear that while the rest of American quilters were indulging in lavish silk and satin crazy quilts during the Victorian era, Amish woman remained faithful to their cotton and wool quilts and only gradually adopted simple patchwork patterns.

"Quilting brought women together and kept them united as a community within the Amish faith," Rose said. "They only adopted new ideas and methods as a group, never as individuals. That's why it took so long for them to introduce patterns like Sunshine and Shadow, which is arguably the most popular and recognizable of Amish patterns, into their designs."

She went to the next quilt, which featured bold primary colored fans against a black background. "This Grandmother's Fan is one of the more radical Amish quilt designs of the thirties, and yet it still incorporates the predominant use of black and disdains prints for solids. The quilters used solid fabrics because some considered printed material a vanity. Although truth be told, I think they also knew how beautifully solid fabrics showed off their quilting stitches."

"What I think is fun is how they made a party out of their activity," Jane said, "getting together to work on a quilt as a group."

Rose nodded. "Since Amish women did most of their quilting during the winter months, it also served as a reason to get out of the house at a time of the year when they normally would not have an opportunity to socialize outside church."

Vera told them how the celebration of the nation's Bicentennial in 1976 had sparked an interest in quilts, as Americans refocused on the art forms of the past and discovered the unique qualities of Amish quilting. "It was then that Amish women began making some quilts to sell in addition to the ones they made for gifts and family use."

"Have you sold any of your work, Mrs. Bellwood?" Laura asked.

"No, unfortunately, I don't have that many completed," she admitted. "Even now that my youngest is in college, working the farm is still a full-time job. As a result I can only do a little bit here and there in the evenings."

"Rose also volunteers at the school where I teach," Vera put in. "She comes in once a week to work with the members of the local 4-H and she teaches a regular craft class."

"I teach fourth graders," Edwina said, clearly pleased to learn that Fred's wife shared her profession.

As the schoolteacher related an amusing tale from her classroom, Jane noticed that Laura Lattimer had drifted away from the group and was closely studying one of Rose's folded quilts with a nine-patch design in gold, brown and olive green.

When she went over to her, Laura gave Jane a somewhat hostile look. "Let me guess. She doesn't want to sell them and I shouldn't ask."

Jane smiled. "Wow, you're a good guesser. Want to tell me how much I weigh or when my birthday is?"

"I get how protective you are of each other in this town," the interior decorator said, sounding exasperated. "I've had three straight days of it. You needn't fuss."

Jane tried to think of something diplomatic to say as she glanced down at the quilt. "That olive green probably isn't your color anyway."

"No, but it would be perfect for a retiring Army general who is moving back from overseas next month and wants his house in perfect order." The younger woman sighed heavily. "I'm no different from any of your other tourists, you know. Except that I *paid* to come here."

"I'm sorry, maybe I misunderstood the whole meaning of this tour," Jane tagged on. "I thought it was to explore homes with classic architecture during the holidays, not clean out the owners."

"Point taken." Oddly, Laura didn't seem insulted. "Look, honey, in my business, you have to be a power buyer or you don't survive. Interior decorators are a dime a dozen in the city, and I have to fight to keep every client. Part of doing that is getting quality merchandise for the lowest price possible."

Jane could sympathize with her on a certain level as the restaurant business wasn't all that different. "You're only looking in one direction, Laura. Private owners aren't the only resources available to you here."

"Your little shops are charming, I'll grant you," she said, making a casual gesture, "but I need household furnishings and accessories, not trinket boxes and home-baked black-berry pies."

"Ah, but you're not from this area, so you don't know the many avenues to serious household stuff. Take quilts, for example. You're only a few miles away from the heart of Amish country." Jane pointed to the window. "If you take that road and head north, in no time you'll see Amish farm-houses with quilts hanging on the front porch rails every mile or so."

"I've heard about that. Are dryers against their religion or something?" She peered at the whirls of Rose's hand stitching again.

"A quilt hanging on the porch means that the lady of the house has handmade quilts to sell." Jane smiled as Laura's gaze snapped up. "It's what you might call the Amish version of direct marketing."

Laura thought for a moment. "Old quilts or new?"

"New for the most part. Sometimes, if a daughter or son is getting married and relocating, both. Each Amish community has its own way of doing things, and it's traditional for a newlywed bride to learn her in-laws' ways of quilting."

"Marvelous." Dollar signs practically popped up in the other woman's eyes. "They probably have no idea of what they're worth."

"Hold on." Jane held up one hand for emphasis. "Just because they're plain people doesn't mean they're naïve. They don't give their quilts away. But you'll get a better price from the maker than you could from a distributor or quilt shop.

"Country lifestyle and decor are very popular here," Jane continued, "and our area markets and shops can provide you with all sorts of antiques and furnishings. Come back again. It's not that long a drive from the city." Jane tried to think of how else she could help the woman. "I love going to browse through the local markets and I've been to some that don't advertise in our town guide. I'll write up a list of them for you."

Laura nodded slowly. "Maybe this trip wasn't a waste of time after all."

Jane heard everyone erupt into mirth behind them and tilted her head. "*Uh-oh*, I think we missed a good joke."

As they rejoined the group, they heard Vera say, "Well, I'll admit I'm glad I didn't have you for a student, Ted. I believe I could tolerate finding frogs or turtles in my desk, but snakes?" She and the others laughed again.

"I keep an empty aquarium in my classroom," Edwina told her, "for just such unexpected visitors."

"What a good solution." Vera was impressed. "I wish I could bring you to our next staff meeting, Edwina."

"Actually, I'm thinking of coming back after the holidays," Edwina said. "If I can get permission from the school board—no small feat there—I'll bring my class with me and make it a field trip." She waited a beat. "Without the animal specimens."

Chapter Fourteen

Since the tour group's driver had still not arrived, Rose sat with the group in the comfortable living room and read a story to her grandsons. Although everyone seemed happy, it was getting late. Jane noticed that Edwina was smothering yawns, Laura was checking her watch every few minutes, and Allan's allergy symptoms appeared to be getting worse. Samuel and Rose also had their son and grandsons staying at the house, and doubtless wanted to get the boys to bed.

Jane decided to call the number that the driver had given to her to see if she could get an update on when to expect the minivan. "Rose, may I use your phone in the kitchen?"

The farmer's wife looked up and smiled. "Certainly."

The line was busy at first, but Jane kept dialing it until she finally got through to the driver, who was still in Potterston.

"I broke down on the way over here and had to call for a tow truck," the man told her. "It appears that the fuel pump is shot. There may be other problems too. The company is having it towed back to headquarters for a mechanic to work on it."

"What should I tell your group?" Jane asked, worried now.

"I called my boss and he's trying to rent a van for me," the driver said. "Problem is with it being so close to Christmas, all of the rental agencies are tapped out. We'll find something, though. It'll just take some time. If you wouldn't mind driving them over, you can leave those folks at that coffee shop in town."

"Sir, the Coffee Shop closed hours ago." Jane glanced out through the window. The wind was picking up and the temperature continued to drop, as it was forecasted to do through the weekend.

"Then they'll have to wait where they are. Make my apologies to the people at the house. I'm doing the best I can."

I can't just dump these people on Rose or in town.

"I'll take them over to my home and let them relax until you can pick them up. Here's the address and phone number." She recited them for him.

"Thank you, miss," the driver said. "I'll call you as soon as I know something."

Jane went back to deliver the news.

"How long did he say it was going to be?" Laura asked, irritated. When Jane told her that the driver couldn't commit to a specific time, the interior decorator shook her head. "This company is such a rinky-dink outfit. I knew I should have booked with someone else."

"We can't impose on Mrs. Bellwood much longer," Ted whispered to Jane. "Would you be able to take us back to town, Ms. Howard?"

"The shops in town are all closed by now, so I thought I'd take you home with me," she said to the group. "I think you'll be more comfortable there, and Grace Chapel Inn is beautiful, if I do say so myself. It'll be like getting a bonus house on the tour."

Edwina's eyebrows drew together. "I hope the driver doesn't take forever. I promised my husband that I'd be home before our son Jack and his family arrive from Arizona. Jack's wife Marcella had my first grandbaby in September. They're coming in tomorrow night, and it will be the first time we get to see little Becky."

"I can't be late getting back to the city, either," Laura said. "I'm throwing a Christmas party for all my clients on Monday. Half my winter budget went into catering and renting a banquet hall, and the deposits are nonrefundable."

"All I want is to go home and *sleep* through Christmas," Allan said. "But I promised my wife that we'd drive up to see my nephew on Christmas Eve. He's a Marine who has been stationed overseas and he's only going to be home on leave for a week."

Ted added his concern, explaining that he and his wife were looking forward to spending their first Christmas together.

Jane felt sorry for the four of them. "I'll call the tour company as soon as we get back to the house." Mentally she crossed her fingers. "I'm sure they'll be able to find a replacement van soon."

After thanking Rose for a wonderful experience, the group went with Jane to Grace Chapel Inn. Even with the car heater running on high, the piercing cold stole everyone's breath away, and by the time they pulled up into the driveway to the inn, a light snow had begun falling.

"Please come into the parlor," Jane told her thoroughly chilled guests as she led them in that direction. "Ted, if you'll turn up the thermostat over by the curio cabinet there, I'll go and make hot drinks and snacks for everyone."

Allan sneezed. "Would you make mine hot tea with lemon, if you have it, Ms. Howard? My throat is starting to feel a bit raw."

"Of course. Here." She picked up a woven plaid blanket and handed it to Allan. "Wrap this around you and take the recliner over there by the heater. It's the warmest and most comfortable spot in the house."

Edwina volunteered to help Jane and went with her to the kitchen. "I would admire your beautiful home, but I think my eyelashes are frozen together," she joked.

"So are mine. When they defrost, I'll probably look around and realize we're in someone else's kitchen." Jane put the kettle on to boil and raided the refrigerator for appropriate offerings. "Whoever she is, she has great taste in vegetables."

Edwina laughed. "Are your sisters at home?"

"No. Alice and Louise are visiting the children's ward at the hospital over in Potterston this evening with our pastor. They throw a Christmas party every year for the kids who can't go home for the holidays."

"The poor dears. You know something, though, I think Max went with them," Edwina said and glanced back at the kitchen door before she added in a lower voice, "I saw him leave the hotel this morning and he was carrying a Santa Claus costume." She giggled.

"No way!" Jane said. "Big Grumpy Max played Santa for the kids?"

The schoolteacher nodded. "I think he might have had some persuasion from that nice pastor of yours."

Jane shook her head in amused disbelief. "I'm beginning to think our pastor could take over a small country if he really wanted to."

Edwina rubbed her hands together and then warmed

them briefly over the stove top. "If it's a warm country, I want to go with him."

The two women worked companionably together until they had a tray of ham and turkey finger sandwiches and strong, hot tea prepared for the group. Jane set the light repast out on the big dining room table while Edwina went to collect everyone. She came back with Ted and Laura, but not Allan.

"Allan's allergy tablets kicked in and he fell asleep in the chair by the fireplace," she explained. "I have the room next to his at our hotel, so I know the poor man was up all last night coughing and sneezing. I thought it best not to disturb him."

"Good idea. We'll let him nap until the driver arrives." Jane excused herself from the group to check the answering machine, but there were no messages.

She turned in time to see Alice, Louise and Max come through the inn door. All three had snow on their coats and hats, and more swirled in behind them on a rush of wind before Alice closed the door.

"Hey, you're just in time for a late supper," Jane said as she came around from behind the reception desk. "I've got sandwiches and hot tea in the dining room."

"Bless you, dear, that sounds like just the thing." Louise shed her coat and hung it on the bentwood rack to dry and then heard voices from the dining room. "Has someone stopped by to visit? I didn't see any car but yours."

"I brought the tour group home with me," Jane said. "Their van broke down and the driver asked me to look after them while he gets a replacement vehicle." She related the rest of what the driver had told her as she accompanied her sisters and Max to the dining room. "I think we should work on finding some alternative transportation," she added in a low voice, meant for Louise's ears only.

"Let me look into that." Louise poured herself a cup of tea and took it and a sandwich with her to the front desk.

Once Max had sat down at the table, Jane coaxed Alice out to the kitchen. "So? What happened?"

"Pastor Thompson got Max to play Santa for the kids," her older sister told her. "Something about a signed baseball pennant of some sort."

"That man knows way too much about temptation." Jane nodded toward the dining room. "How did it go with Santa in there?"

"It was an amazing thing to watch, Jane. He's such a big, loud man, and yet he was so gentle and kind to the children." Alice rolled her eyes. "Then he swore Louise and me to secrecy about it. He doesn't want the others to know for some reason."

"Edwina suspects him, but I don't believe the others

know." Jane thought that she understood why. She personally felt that doing things for others was the important thing, not taking credit for doing them. Max probably felt the same way. "Ruins his gruff, old businessman image, though, doesn't it?"

"Totally wrecked it for me." Alice took Jane's hands in hers. "This is partly your fault, you know. It was your suggestion about treating him like a cranky patient that led to this."

Jane thought about the phone call that she was expecting at any minute and squeezed her sister's hands. "Here's hoping it leads to a lot more."

Louise first contacted the tour company, whose service manager was working on subcontracting a bus to pick up and take the five visitors home. Unfortunately, it wasn't looking very promising.

"This tour was the last of the season. All of our other minivans have been sent upstate for annual maintenance," the manager told her. "We're hoping to obtain a suitable vehicle from one of the regional car rental companies, but you know what it's like at this time of night and with the holiday coming up. They don't have anything available."

"I sympathize with your dilemma, but you are responsible for these people," Louise said, feeling a little alarmed at how casual the man sounded.

"I'll see if I can get someone to make a run out there and take them over to their hotel for the night."

"That will not be necessary. My sisters and I will be happy to drive them back." She sighed. "You are not going to leave them in that hotel for the holidays, are you?"

"At this point, ma'am, I really can't say. I'm doing the best I can," he said. "That's all anyone can expect."

Louise, who had hoped for better results, ended the call and sighed in frustration. It was possible that the group could call relatives, but she hated the idea of people driving out to Grace Chapel Inn during the night and under such nasty weather conditions. The roads were sure to be very icy within the next hour.

After thinking for a minute, she remembered a local travel agent with whom she had often done business. Louise thought that she probably would not object to being called at home, so she picked up the phone and dialed the agent's number. She explained the situation and asked for the other woman's advice.

"I know that tour company. They're reputable, but they have a small operation, so don't expect any miracles from them."

Louise silently counted to ten. "Is there any alternative that I can offer to these people?"

"Let me see what's open." The agent checked her computer, and confirmed that all of the seats on trains and buses were sold out until December 28. "I can put your group on a waiting list for any seats that become available and check the independent charter services."

"That would be immensely helpful, Janice, thank you." She looked up to see Laura Lattimer approaching.

"Don't thank me yet, Louise," Janice told her. "It's a long shot. I think you might want to prepare those folks for the worst-case scenario. They might not be going home for Christmas."

Louise closed her eyes briefly. The very last thing she wanted was to leave these people in an unfamiliar hotel for the holidays, but surely no one would expect her and her sisters to look after them.

Since Laura was listening, she simply thanked the agent and ended the call. "I'm sorry to keep you waiting. What can I do for you?"

"You can tell me that the bus driver is on his way here to pick us up."

Louise wasn't going to tell her how bleak the situation looked. "The tour company is still making the arrangements, so my sisters and I will be taking your group back to your hotel."

Laura must have seen something in her expression, however, for she planted her hands on her hips. "They're going to dump us here, aren't they? No, don't bother to answer. I'm calling my attorney. This time, I'm suing. By the time I get through, I will *own* that tour company." She pulled her cell phone out of her purse and stalked off.

Louise took a sip of her tea, which had grown cold. Hope was fading fast, and she did not relish the prospect of telling the group that they faced the possibility of being stranded.

She should not have to be the one to tell them. She should be enjoying her vacation with her sisters. *I knew this would turn out to be a disaster. I knew it, and I went ahead and let myself be drawn into it.*

For a moment she felt like calling her sisters together and giving them both a good talking-to. It was one thing to help people, but quite another to be made responsible for them. She should never have let Jane and Alice get involved with this group.

Her Bible sat on the desk next to the phone, with the bookmark where she had left off reading the night before. At the time, she had been thinking of Eliot and missing him. She picked it up and opened it to Philippians 4:6–7, a verse that had always given her such comfort, and began to read.

"Do not be anxious about anything, but in everything, by prayer and petition, with thanksgiving, present your requests to God. And the peace of God, which transcends all understanding, will guard your hearts and your minds in Christ Jesus."

I know You understand, Lord. I suspect You have been mankind's travel agent from the minute Adam and Eve left the Garden. But why is this happening to us? We deserved our vacation and we gave up part of it to help these people. Was that not enough? A fresh surge of resentment welled up inside her. *When is it enough, Lord?*

She continued to read the chapter through the thirteenth verse, hoping it would dispel some of the anger and resentment she felt.

"I know what it is to be in need and I know what it is to have plenty. I have learned the secret of being content in any and every situation, whether well fed or hungry, whether living in plenty or in want. I can do everything through him who gives me strength."

Louise had gradually been blessed with contentment after a time of loneliness and despair, thanks to her sisters and the Lord. It was that contentment that she wanted to guard and not have disturbed by these five strangers. She had always felt very strongly that holidays were for family.

Resentment still twisted inside her, unwilling to let go. The sensible thing to do would be to take them back to their hotel and let them sort out what to do by themselves. Laura Lattimer would definitely enjoy shouting at the company employees and at her attorney over the phone. But the group was not responsible for what had happened to them and they would probably not have any better luck than she had had in finding transportation.

They would have to make the best of it. Max had no one to go home to, so he would probably not care much. Edwina struck Louise as the type of woman who could whip up a Christmas party with some chips and candy bars from a vending machine; she would look after Allan. The never-satisfied Laura had her cellular phone, pending lawsuit and electronic gadgets to keep her busy. Even Ted could use the time to sort out how he wanted to put together his portfolio.

The hotel would see to their physical needs and they had telephones. They could call and speak to their families. That would have to be enough.

Louise glanced at her calendar. The group was supposed to leave for home the next day, so all they would need to do was extend their reservations. She froze as a thought occurred to her.

If they could be extended.

All week Louise had been turning down requests for accommodations from people coming to Potterston for two conventions and a regional parade—not to mention the usual travelers arriving to visit their relatives in the area.

Quickly she dialed the hotel in Potterston and asked to be connected to the reservations clerk, who confirmed her worst fears.

"I'm sorry, Mrs. Smith, but we're booked straight through until New Year's Day," the clerk told her.

"These people have no transportation. They won't be able to leave."

"I'm sorry to hear that. I've been checking the other hotels in the area for available rooms and they're in the same situation. Let me ask my manager." The clerk put her on hold and then came back to the phone. "My manager, um, says that the folks in your group will have to check out tomorrow morning by eleven."

"You intend to throw them out onto the street? In this weather?" Louise asked, incredulous.

The clerk put her on hold for another minute. "My manager says that if they have no place else to go, they can stay at the town shelter. I'm really sorry, Mrs. Smith."

That put the finishing touch on the disaster. By the next afternoon the five visitors would have no place to stay except a shelter for the homeless.

These people are in terrible straits, Louise thought. *I have my family and my home, while they are far away from theirs.*

Alice arrived carrying a mug of tea, and at Louise's inquiring glance, she lifted it and smiled. "I thought you might need another cup."

It was as simple as that, Louise realized, and felt all her resentment disappear. When you thought someone was in need, you provided what you could to help to ease her burden. It might be something as small as a cup of hot tea or as important as shelter from the cold.

Her Aunt Ethel's words came back to her at that moment. "A Christian home keeps a candle burning in the window through Christmas Eve to light the way of the Holy Family, as well as to welcome guests."

"Thank you, dear." Louise accepted the tea and marveled at the sense of peace she felt as she let go of the resentment that had been her companion. "What would you think of inviting our tour group to stay with us until they can make arrangements to get home?"

Chapter Fifteen

*E*ven after their talk, Alice could not believe that Louise was volunteering to put up the tour group at the inn until they could find a way home. Her older sister had been so adamant about taking their vacation time for themselves and now she was giving it away. She even seemed happy about doing it.

"We must be practical," Louise said. "Given the circumstances, it's really the only thing to do."

"Couldn't we drive them to the next nearest city?" Alice asked. "I'm sure there have to be some hotels available in Lancaster."

"I think our guests would prefer to stay here instead of being shuffled off to another strange hotel." Louise glanced at her Bible for a moment. "I feel very strongly about this, Alice. It's the right thing to do."

The group had various reactions to Louise's suggestion.

"It would only be for a day or two, right?" Ted asked

hopefully. "Until the new van gets here or we can contact our families?"

"I wouldn't count on the van," Max muttered in his gloomy way.

"I'm grateful, of course, Louise, but do you have enough room for the five of us?" Edwina asked. "I would share with Laura, if that would help."

"I'm a terribly light sleeper," Laura said and folded her arms defensively when everyone looked at her. "It's true. Even the slightest sound wakes me up. I can't help it."

Alice saw the way Louise looked at the younger woman, this time with more pity than exasperation. She was tempted to ask Laura how well she would sleep in a homeless shelter, then felt a surge of guilt for the unkind thought.

No, she decided, *if Louise can be graceful about this, then so can I.*

Ted pushed his glasses up higher on the bridge of his nose before he glanced around the room. "I'd share with Allan, but I think he needs his own room so that he can rest undisturbed."

Max regarded the younger man. "Well, I can't share a room with you."

"I wouldn't be a bother, sir," Ted said, flushing a little. "I'm a very quiet person."

"That's not the issue. This is." The businessman tapped the bump on his prominent nose. "I had it broken when I was a boy and I've snored like a freight train ever since. My wife had to wear earplugs. Unless you have some, *you* wouldn't be able to sleep."

"There is no need for any of you to share," Louise said, startling Alice again. "We have four empty guest rooms, and I or one of my sisters will give up one of our bedrooms to provide the fifth."

Jane frowned at their older sister for a moment, clearly surprised at her sudden and complete turnaround. "It may only be for one night. The tour company could show up with a new van tomorrow."

"I may be able to get in touch with my brother, if he hasn't left town for our parents' house yet," Ted said. "He may be willing to give some of the rest of you a ride into the city."

Since Louise was sacrificing her long-anticipated holiday and Jane would be cooking for everyone, Alice decided to make her own contribution.

"I'll give up my room and sleep on a folding bed," she volunteered. "Jane, do you mind if I double up with you? Your room is a little bigger than Louise's."

Her younger sister nodded. "Sounds good to me. We can sneak down and have a midnight feast together after Louise goes to sleep."

"No pizza," their oldest sister said in her severest tone, even as approval glowed in her eyes. "No ice cream."

Laura scanned their faces, her own expression uncertain now. "You three are talking like this is going to be some kind of schoolgirl adventure."

"Why not let it be an adventure?" Jane asked. "We can't change the situation and it's better than being unhappy."

"We've all been so disappointed that we really haven't thought about the other side of this," Ted said, looking at the rest of the group, trying not to sound as glum as before, "We're forgetting that these ladies also had holiday plans and now we're spoiling those plans."

Laura looked uncomfortable. "Are we ruining your Christmas?"

Alice summoned a smile. "How can a house full of people at the holidays be a bad thing?"

Alice thought Max might jump in and start complaining along with Laura about the inconvenience of it all, but oddly the businessman remained quiet.

"Ms. Lattimer, we'll try to make the best of it." Alice said. "That's all any of us can do."

"It will be if we don't get a change of clothes." Edwina tugged at her sweater. "I don't think I share the same size with anyone here, so I wouldn't even be able to borrow something from you other ladies."

"My little car isn't very trustworthy on icy roads, but if Louise will lend me her Cadillac, I'll drive all of you over to your hotel to check out tonight," Jane said. "You can get your cases then."

"If that van doesn't get here tomorrow, my holiday and my business are going to be ruined." Laura was staring at the snow falling outside the window. "Are you sure there's nothing we can do? No one we can call? What if we end up being stuck here through Christmas? What are we going to do?"

Alice thought she sounded a little desperate and went over to place a hand gently on her shoulder. "You'll help us celebrate it, Laura."

⌒

Jane took everyone but Allan Hansford, whose items Ted promised to retrieve, off to Potterston to check out of the hotel, while Alice and Louise prepared what was needed for their unexpected guests. The rooms were clean and prepared for the guests that they had booked for after the holidays, but the bathrooms needed to be stocked with the towels and complimentary toiletries that they provided for guests. Then there were menus to consider and supplies to check.

When they returned from Potterston, their new guests needed to make calls to their families to let them know where they were and what had happened.

Unfortunately, the families were unable to help the stranded group. Ted's brother had already left to visit their parents, and as Ted didn't have snow tires on his own car, the long drive was too dangerous for his wife to make. Edwina's husband had to stay home to be on hand to pick up their son's family and other relatives from the airport. Allan's wife couldn't come to pick up her husband since she had stopped driving several years before because of poor eyesight.

"What about Laura?" Alice asked Louise.

"She has been trying to contact someone," Louise said.

In fact, Laura Lattimer's attempts to reach her attorney, her mother, or anyone else who could drive to Acorn Hill to pick her up drained her cell phone's battery. The very next morning she went downstairs early and began monopolizing the inn's phone for much of the day.

"I only want to call the office again and see if my secretary was able to reach my mother," she told Edwina when the schoolteacher said something to her about it. "She wouldn't have gone to Europe for the holidays. She hates the Continent in winter."

"You've already phoned her at least a half dozen times since last night, Laura." Edwina sighed. "I don't think the answer is going to be any different."

Through it all, Louise remained rock-steady and serene. That afternoon, she met in the kitchen with her sisters to plan strategy. "Alice, if you would put out clean towels for everyone, I will recheck supplies and supervise telephone calls." She glanced at Jane. "Would you like someone to help you with dinner?"

"You're going to stick me with 'Lady Lattimer,' aren't you?" When her older sister nodded, she sighed and squared her shoulders. "All right. I'll talk about lofts in San Francisco and make her chop celery. Or maybe I'll tie her up, gag her and toss her in the corner."

"Lofts," Louise said firmly. "Celery. Nothing more."

Jane had just put together the ingredients for dinner when Ted came into the kitchen. "Hi, Ted. What's up?"

"I'm your substitute helper," he said. "Miss Lattimer developed a sudden migraine and had to go lie down for a few hours."

She raised her eyebrows. "Is she all right?"

He cleared his throat. "I'd say she's just very, very frustrated. She's called her mother over and over, but so far, no answer."

"That's awful."

"The thing is, I don't think she's as upset over not reaching her mother as she is about the tour company. I think she's used to having a certain amount of control over the business side of her life. So being unable to get around this problem"—he spread out his hands— "is probably a whole new experience for her."

"I hope it turns out to be a good one." She glanced at his hands. "How are you at chopping veggies?"

He gave one bunch of celery a pained look. "About as skilled as I am at piloting the space shuttle."

"No problem. We'll just keep you away from NASA and my kitchen knives, and make you use your hands. Speaking of which, would you mind washing up at the sink?"

After Ted had scrubbed his hands, Jane brought over a big salad bowl and two washed heads of iceberg lettuce, one of which she handed to him.

"First, you remove the stem, like so." She slammed the lettuce stem-side down on the counter, then turned it over and easily popped out the wide, flat stem section.

"Wow!" Ted imitated her with nearly the exact same results. "That's a neat trick."

"We chefs know a million of them. Just don't slam too hard, or you'll only have pulp left and have to make veggie juice. Now, you insert your thumbs here"—she showed him the place at the top of the lettuce—"and rip it in two."

Ted was successful in dividing the head into two halves. "Why don't you use a knife to do this?"

"You can use a knife, but tearing it up this way makes the lettuce appear more appetizing. It's also a terrific way to work out frustration, as is the stem removal part." She set the bowl in front of him. "Now, you tear the halves into quarters, and the quarters into eighths, then separate the eighths and toss them in the bowl. Tear up any big pieces that are not bite-sized. While you do that, I'm going to whip up our entrée."

Ted went to work on the lettuce. "Cooking seems like fun."

"Why do you think most chefs are guys?" She chuckled at his expression. "It's true, you know. Real men really can cook."

"We can burn things too."

Jane's quickest version of beef stroganoff was simmering by the time Ted finished the lettuce and set the dining room table, so she had time to show him how to chop the other vegetables for the salad and mix up homemade vinaigrette dressing.

"I like making my own dressings versus store-bought," she told him as she poured a measure of red wine vinegar into the shaker bottle. "No chemicals, no preservatives, and I decide which ingredients to use. You make just enough for the meal and then you don't have bottles of dressing sitting in the fridge either."

"I wish my wife Linda was here," he said unexpectedly. "This is her kind of cooking. She loves spontaneity and surprises. I know she would really like you and your sisters."

Jane gave him a sympathetic smile. "Were you able to get hold of her?"

He nodded.

Maybe getting him to talk about it would help. "Was she disappointed?"

"Not very. In fact, Linda was great on the phone." He hunched his shoulders. "She said that calendars don't run our lives and that if I get stranded here for the holidays, then Christmas would be the day I come home."

"Sounds like you married the right woman." She went over to check and stir the stroganoff mixture.

"I know I did." He ducked his head and his voice went low. "I don't deserve her, you know. Linda is such a good, loving person. I can't even afford to give her a proper home."

"Yet." Jane gave him a sympathetic look. "Professional freelance photographers make good money, Ted. Don't give up on that."

"Do you know that she insisted that I spend my Christmas bonus on this trip? Even with my bonus, I could only afford to go alone, but she didn't care." He took off his glasses and used his handkerchief to polish the lenses. Without them on, he looked very young and unsure of himself. "That's the kind of person she is. She told me that I could take some fabulous pictures on this tour and that building my portfolio was more important to her than a fancy gift or big dinner."

"She's investing in your future." Jane felt admiration. "That in itself is a gift."

"I know, but it was still so hard to leave her behind. Now I might miss our first Christmas together." He put his glasses back on, but they didn't hide the sadness in his eyes. "But like Linda, I'll have to make the best of it." He glanced around. "Now what can I do?"

Jane smiled. "Let me introduce you to the immense pleasure to be had in sautéing garlic and shallots."

Jane's delicious beef stroganoff was received with enthusiasm and the appetizing fare went a long way to improving the atmosphere over dinner.

"We do appreciate you ladies providing accommodations for us," Edwina said. "I know you weren't expecting five houseguests to drop in like this."

"It's the nicest thing that's happened on this trip," Laura murmured, then looked up with a guilty expression. "I'm also grateful."

"So am I," Ted chimed in. "Thank you, ladies."

Max frowned. "Will the tour company be reimbursing you for the expense of putting us up?"

"Yes, the manager was quite happy to do so," Jane assured him. "There will be no charge to any of you either. They're taking full responsibility for the cost and we're still hoping they'll find a van for you all."

Louise brought up the subject of holiday dishes, and all

the guests talked about things they liked to cook and their favorite recipes for the holidays. Only Laura seemed pale and depressed, and after picking at her food excused herself from the table to return to her room.

"You know," Jane said, her tone thoughtful as she watched the interior decorator depart, "Laura didn't mention anything about her family."

"Does she have anyone?" Max asked.

"She said she was planning to visit her mother after the business party she's giving on Monday," Edwina said, "although I got the impression that they're not very close and evidently her mother has gone off somewhere without telling Laura."

"Not very thoughtful of her," Ted said.

Max's expression turned melancholy. "At least she has someone to visit."

When the rest of the group had finished and Louise and Alice had begun to collect the dishes, Edwina insisted that she clean up after dinner.

"I know my way around a kitchen, and you ladies have done enough for us today," the schoolteacher said firmly. "Ted, would you check on Allan? Max can help me with the dishes."

Alice rose to her feet. "I'll go up with you, Ted."

"Would you ask our patient if he'd like some dinner?" Jane asked. "I can make up a tray for him if he's feeling hungry."

Alice nodded. To Ted, she said, "Let me get my medical bag so I can give him a quick check-over while I'm up there."

After she retrieved her bag from the front closet, she accompanied Ted to the second floor. "Do you know what Allan is allergic to?" she asked.

"He mentioned pollen and that he suffers a lot during the summer." Ted thought for a minute. "You know, now that I think about it, he started feeling ill just after we visited Mayor Tynan's home. That big, dried-flower wreath on the inside of his door might have triggered this."

"That could be it. Pollen is a catalyst whether it's from fresh flowers or dried ones." Alice knocked on the door of the Sunrise Room. "Allan? May Ted and I come in?"

There was the sound of coughing, then a muffled, "Yes."

Louise had put Allan in the Sunrise Room, probably in hopes that the bright color scheme of yellow, white and blue would cheer him up. It was Grace Chapel Inn's unofficial "sick" guest room.

When Alice saw his watery eyes and reddened nose, and heard the congested sound of his breathing, she set down her case and took out her stethoscope.

"Allan, if you have no objections, I'd like to check you over," she said as he sat up. "I'm a registered nurse, but if your condition requires a hospital visit, we need to take you there."

"I don't mind at all, although I look about as good as I feel," he told her. "My prescription allergy tablets are at home and the over-the-counter medication I bought yesterday isn't helping much."

Ted excused himself so that Alice could examine Allan with privacy.

After a quick check and some questions about his medical history, she found that aside from the discomfort of his sinus congestion, the older man was in very good health.

"Your heart rate and blood pressure are fine." She released the pressure cuff from his forearm and tucked it back in her case, then took out a lighted scope to check his eyes, ears and airways. "Still, if you feel dizzy, or your symptoms change or get worse, I want you to tell me right away."

"I will." Allan looked over at the snow falling outside the window and his expression turned sad.

"Is there something you want to talk about?" Alice asked carefully.

"It's my nephew. He should be flying over the Atlantic right about now. He's been stationed in the Middle East for almost two years. We were really looking forward to spending his leave with him and his parents."

Alice placed her hand over his. "It's possible that the tour company may still come through and send a new van."

"I have the feeling that's not going to happen. It's all right." He turned his head away to sneeze. "He'll be with his parents and my wife. Knowing that is almost as good as seeing him myself." He reached for a tissue and blew his nose.

"I have some nasal spray you can use along with your tablets," Alice said. "You should take a warm shower, too, and have some soup. That will help open up your sinus passages a bit more and make you feel better."

He settled back on the pillows. "The only thing that will make me feel better is a magic carpet ride home." He glanced at her bag. "I don't suppose you have one of those in there I could borrow."

She smiled at his humor. "If I did, you'd have a five-way fight for it. I'm afraid you'll have to settle for my sister's homemade chicken soup."

Chapter Sixteen

Once Max and Edwina were busy in the kitchen, Louise asked Jane to join her in the parlor and closed the door so they could speak privately.

"I just received another phone call from the tour company," she said. "They have not found a van and they don't think that they will now."

"Wonderful." Jane rubbed a hand over her face.

"The manager will call me again tomorrow, but the company's office has now closed and will not be reopening until after Christmas." Louise gave her a grave look. "Jane, their families are unable to help, either. I think we must either come up with transportation for them ourselves or plan on providing accommodations for the group through Christmas."

"Oh boy!" Jane dropped onto the sofa. "That is not the news they're expecting to hear." She rested her elbows against her knees and propped her chin on her fists. "Okay, I say we just forget about the tour company and drive them home ourselves."

Louise nodded. "That was my thought. With five peo-ple, two drivers and all their luggage, we will need two cars. You know how I hate driving in snow. Do you think you and Alice could take them tomorrow?"

"Of course we can. My car might be a tad small, but if you'll lend me your Cadillac again, we should be fine." Jane studied her face. "There's something else, isn't there? More bad news."

"Yes. I listened to the weather report and there is a large storm front moving in from the Midwest. It has brought blizzard conditions to central Ohio and shut down parts of the interstate there."

"Just when you think it can't get any worse...."

"It very well may." Louise came over and rested a hand on her shoulder. "If you and Alice leave first thing in the morning, you should be able to reach the city before the storm arrives. However, it is very likely that you will not be able to return home until it passes through."

Jane felt bitterness rise inside her. "So you'll probably spend the holidays alone here while we're stuck in Philly. Or we can stay home and be together while they're miser-able and stranded here away from *their* families."

"That seems to be the choice."

"The choices really stink." Jane rested her head back against the cushions. "This is one of those God tests Alice is always talking about, isn't it? One of us has to make a sacrifice."

Louise came to sit down next to her. "These people need to go home for Christmas, Jane. I don't want to be separated from you or Alice, so I know how they feel. I know I could not enjoy our holiday, knowing that we could have reunited them with their families."

Jane met her sister's bright gaze.

"Alice and I are your sisters. We love you." Louise wiped a tear away from Jane's cheek. "Whether we're together or apart, that will never change."

Jane nodded, unable to speak.

"Good." Louise kissed her forehead and then looked back into her eyes. "Now, are you sure you can do this? That you *want* to do this?"

She nodded. "I know Alice will agree it's the best decision."

"Then let's go and talk to her, and we'll tell the others in the morning at breakfast."

$\backsim$

"How is Allan?" Max asked Alice when she came back down to the kitchen.

"Uncomfortable, but otherwise in good spirits." Alice went to the freezer and took out a container of Jane's chicken soup. "Well, not really good spirits. I think that would be too much to ask of anyone, under the circumstances."

"Edwina looked done in, so I told her to go upstairs and get some sleep." Max finished loading the last dish into the dishwasher before closing its door and starting the wash cycle. He seemed completely at ease in the kitchen, something that Alice had not expected. "You might want to plan for what you'll need if the power fails."

"I will have to listen to the weather report." Alice took down a soup bowl from the cabinet. "You don't seem to be very upset about being stranded here, Max."

"I'm not," he said in his blunt way. "I'd have gone back to an empty house and spent Christmas by myself, the way I have for the last ten years. Being stranded in a house full of people isn't so bad."

"Do you have to be alone?" Alice put the soup in the microwave to heat.

"No one has to be alone." He opened a cabinet and looked inside, then placed several spice jars inside on the shelf. "With me, it just worked out that way."

"I know this is none of my business, but if you were given the chance, would you reconcile with your son?"

"It would never happen." Max made a dismissive gesture. "My son made his sentiments clear to me after his mother died, and he's never made an effort to change his ways or see my point of view. I haven't seen him since her funeral, in fact. I'm not part of his life anymore."

"What if your son thinks the same way about you?" Alice asked gently. "He could think that you made your feelings clear and that you've never made the effort to change your ways or see his point of view, so that he's not a part of your life."

Max was silent for so long that Alice thought she might have seriously offended him.

Just before she opened her mouth to apologize, he said, "No, don't go and spoil it now with some female twittering. You could be right. He could feel the same way as I do. We always did think alike." There was a note of pride in his last words.

That is his greatest obstacle, Alice realized, *his pride.* "You might consider then taking the first step toward reconciliation yourself."

He seemed defeated again. "After a decade of silence between us? How would you cross that kind of chasm?"

"A voice can often be heard from a great distance. Call your son, Max. Talk to him. Tell him a fantastic story about being stranded by a snowstorm in a little town in Pennsylvania." Alice brought a tray out from a cabinet under the counter and placed a bowl on it for the steaming soup. "Tell him that you'd like to see him."

He gave her a long, silent look. "Do you really think that is all that it would take, after all these years apart?"

"I don't know." She had to be honest. "What is the worst that can happen? He says no or he hangs up the telephone."

He stiffened. "A man has his pride."

"Yes. You both do." She tilted her head. "Is your pride more important than your son?"

"I thought it was, once," Max admitted. "Perhaps I was wrong." He glanced at her. "You say pride like it was a bad thing."

"Pride is one of the sins we Christians battle against every day," Alice said. "We feel entitled to our pride, because it seems that we have worked so hard for it."

He gave her one of his scowls. "I have worked very hard for what I have. That's nothing to sneeze at. My son turned his back on everything I taught him in order to chase a foolish dream."

"He hurt your pride with his own. He made his choice at the expense of your dreams for him."

"Yes, he—" Max stopped for a moment. "No, that's not how it was." Suddenly, he looked pained. "My son wanted me to understand his art. He tried to talk to me. I didn't want to accept it and I drove him away." He shook his head. "I drove him away from me."

"Max, in the Bible it says, 'Do nothing out of selfish

ambition or vain conceit, but in humility consider others better than yourselves. Each of you should look not only to your own interests, but also to the interests of others. Your attitude should be the same as that of Christ Jesus: Who, being in very nature God, did not consider equality with God something to be grasped, but made himself nothing, taking the very nature of a servant, being made in human likeness. And being found in appearance as a man, he humbled himself and became obedient to death—even death on a cross!' [Philippians 2:3–8].

"I memorized that passage a long time ago because I have always regarded it to be the ultimate pride cruncher. When I remember that the Son of God humbled Himself to become a servant of man and died for our sakes, then any pride I might be tempted to let rule my heart shrinks until I can clearly see how petty and small it is."

He released a long, slow breath. "You make a convincing argument, Alice. Very well. After I get back home, I'll take the first step. I'll track down my son and I'll call him. Who knows, maybe he won't hang up on me for a few minutes. And, Alice . . . thank you."

Once their five guests were settled in their rooms and Allan had been served his soup, the Howard sisters retired for the evening. Louise reminded Jane to set her alarm clock so that they could get an early start on preparing for their trip in the morning.

Since Alice had slept on the folding bed in Jane's room the night before, her younger sister offered to trade places with her.

"I don't want you up tossing and turning like you did last night," Jane told her. "You know me. I can sleep on a rock."

"Nonsense. I'm a nurse, I can sleep standing up. Which beats your rock." Alice turned down the folding bed's sheets and arranged the thick, lavender thermal blanket she had put at the foot. She eyed the rather flat pillow that she had found so uncomfortable the night before. "However, if you wouldn't mind parting with one of your bed pillows, my neck and I would be eternally grateful."

Jane startled her by tossing the pillow at her. "We never had a pillow fight when we were girls, did we?"

"I was in my twenties when you were a girl," Alice reminded her. "Which is a good thing, because I think you would have dragged me into one scrape after another."

"I've never looked at you and Louise as being older than me, you know. I never even noticed the age differences except on your birthdays, when Father counted out all those hundreds of candles." She ducked in time to avoid the pillow Alice threw back at her and laughed. "You have to be faster than that."

"If we make too much noise, Louise will have something to say about it," Alice warned her.

Jane nodded and handed the pillow back to her. "Do you ever miss it, Alice? Being a kid?"

"It was easier to enjoy things for what they are." Alice recalled the conversation they had had about Jane's memories of Christmas and how she had promised to make this one special for her younger sister. "I know this isn't what you wanted for the holidays, but I know Father would be very proud of us."

"I hope so, because it's going to be really hard to leave Louise here by herself tomorrow." Jane climbed into bed and thumped her pillow a few times before curling up on her side. "Good night, Alice."

"Sweet dreams, dear."

Despite her reassurances to Jane, sleeping on the folding bed for Alice was only marginally more comfortable than taking a nap standing up. She tried not to toss and turn, but as soon as Jane fell asleep, she tried to find a more restful position. She was used to the firm support of her own mattress, so the thin one on the folding bed seemed flimsy in comparison.

I feel like I'm lying on cardboard, Alice thought as she turned onto her back and stared through the darkness at the ceiling. *At least now I'm getting firsthand experience of how it might feel for some guest to sleep on this thing. I'll have to talk to Louise about getting a better mattress.*

"Make a wish."

"*Hmm?*" Alice lifted her head and looked over at Jane, who had rolled onto her opposite side. "Did you say something?"

"You wanted me to make a wish," Jane repeated in a strange voice. "I want to hear him again."

"Who, dear?"

"Father." Jane sighed.

Alice frowned as she sat up. Her vision had adjusted to the darkness, so she could see that Jane's eyes were closed. In addition, she could hear that her voice had become high-pitched and her words a little slurred.

Jane was talking in her sleep.

"What about Father, Jane?" she asked, keeping her voice low so that she wouldn't wake her.

"I miss him." Jane rolled over and buried her face in her pillow for a moment.

Alice felt tears sting her eyes. "But Father is with the Lord now, sweetheart."

"I know." Jane sighed again, then murmured, "Christmas gifts should be special, but you can't bring our father back.

He's in heaven now and I'll never hear his voice again." She made a low, sad sound. "And we could never afford the snow-plow for Max."

Max needed a *snowplow?* Alice decided that had to be some strange element from Jane's dream. "So what you want for Christmas is to hear your father's voice again?"

"It's okay." Jane smiled in her sleep. "I hear him in my dreams."

Chapter Seventeen

The next morning the Howard sisters woke up early so that they could prepare to pack up their guests and take them back to the city.

As usual, Jane was the first one up and the first to discover that the weather forecast had been wrong. Wendell came downstairs with her and jumped up on the counter, when a low whistling sound drew Jane to the window over the sink.

Fred's prediction had been correct.

Outside Jane could see nothing but a grayish darkness and snow, snow that was falling so rapidly that she could actually watch it piling up against the windowpanes. It was so thick and heavy that it blocked out everything on the inn property and whirled past the window so fast that watching it was like staring into a TV screen filled with static. The faint whistling sound was growing louder, too, indicating that the wind was increasing.

There was no possibility of driving the group back to the city now.

"Well, that settles that," she told the family cat as she stroked his head.

Alice came down dressed for their trip and smiled at Jane.

"Are the birds finally taking advantage of our feeders?" she asked, nodding toward the window.

"I can't see the bird feeders," Jane said. "Or the birds. Or the trees." She stepped away so Alice could see the conditions outside.

"Oh no!" Alice was shocked by the severity of what she beheld. She pressed a hand against the cold pane, as if not sure that what she was seeing was real. "The forecaster said the front wouldn't reach here until this afternoon."

Jane turned on the radio and tuned it to the all-news station. As she made coffee and tea for breakfast, the latest weather report broadcast reached them.

The news was grim. Nearly a foot of snow had already fallen and, combined with high winds, had created hazardous conditions. A severe-weather advisory had been issued for travelers, warning against using the interstate and other major roads for anything but emergencies.

Louise joined them in time to hear the report and went to the window. She stood staring out at the snow for so long that Jane grew worried.

"Louise?" She put a hand on her older sister's arm. "You okay?"

"I was just thinking how fortunate it is that we didn't tell the guests about our plans last night." She leaned against Jane for a moment. "They would be so disappointed, having their hopes raised, only to wake up to . . ." she gestured toward the falling snow.

So you'll be disappointed for them. Jane patted her sister's shoulder before taking a deep breath. "There is a reason for everything that happens. Let's make the most of it."

As she was making breakfast, Jane took a moment to call the carriage house and check on their aunt to see if she needed anything. Ethel Buckley had been the wife of a farmer and was accustomed to getting up at dawn, so she answered the phone after only one ring.

"I'm fine, dear, except for hearing on the radio that church services have been canceled." Her aunt sounded anything but fine. "Are you girls all right?"

"We have a full house." Jane told her about the tour group becoming stranded at the inn. "Have you heard from Lloyd? Alice told me he had come down with the flu."

"He went to see the doctor over in Potterston yesterday and decided to stay overnight with that fishing buddy of his," Ethel told her. "I expect he's stuck there now, and him sicker than a dog."

That explained her aunt's sounding depressed: Jane knew Ethel had had her heart set on spending the holidays with her beau.

Is anyone going to have a happy Christmas?

"Why don't you come up to the house when the storm dies down?" she asked her aunt. "We could use another happy face around here. They're in short supply."

"A face I can bring," her aunt said. "Happy I won't promise. I'll rig a storm line when I do, though." She referred to an old farmer's trick of tying a rope to one building and reeling it out until it could be tied to another building. It kept people from getting lost in the blinding snow and winds of a blizzard.

Jane said good-bye and hung up the phone. She flipped the last of her raspberry pancakes onto the stack that she had already made and brought them to the table.

"Add one more person to the cheer-up roster." She told her sisters about Lloyd's unhappy situation and her invitation to Ethel.

"It's a shame we can't call someone and request that Christmas be postponed for a week." Alice passed the pitcher of maple syrup to Louise. "That would solve so many problems."

"We could call FEMA, maybe," Jane said, "and have this section of Pennsylvania declared a disaster area, get an extra week to dig out of the snow and unite people who should be together for the holidays."

"FEMA is for tornadoes and floods, dear," Louise said, "not snowstorms and family separations."

Alice sighed. "I think it's starting to depress me now."

"Some vacation, *huh*?" Jane reached out and took hold of both her sisters' hands. "I'm the cause of this and I am truly sorry. I never saw this happening."

"You aren't allowed to carry all the culpability," Louise told her. "I invited them to stay with us." She looked across the table at Alice. "I'm sure you had something to do with it too."

Their middle sister nodded. "I was a conspirator from the beginning. I should have at least one-third share of the blame."

Jane couldn't hide her relief or her love for her sisters. "Okay, so what do we do now?"

"We should get everyone into the spirit of things," Alice suggested. "Maybe we could put on some Christmas music and bake cookies? Have a decorate-the-inn party?"

"I hope that our guests might be up for that kind of activity. How is Mr. Hansford doing?" Louise asked.

"He is going to need at least a full day of bed rest, maybe two," Alice said. "He's in good shape, but I'll keep a close eye on him, just to be sure."

"Max seemed pretty chipper last night," Jane said, eyeing her. "Did you have something to do with that?"

"I talked him into calling his son after the holidays. They haven't spoken for ten years—it's about time that they did." Alice flushed a little as both her sisters stared at her. "It's not as hard to cheer up someone who already has no one at home. Truth be told, I think Max is happy that this happened. He even said it was better to be stranded here with us than to go home and sit in an empty house."

"One down, four to go . . . five counting Aunt Ethel." Jane held out the plate of pancakes so that her sisters could take seconds. "I tried to cheer up Ted while we were working on dinner."

Alice perked up. "How did that go?"

"Terrible. I only ended up depressing him more." She thought for a moment. "I think it was talking about his wife that upset him. Maybe we should try to avoid the subject of family altogether."

"I know that they are upset over being separated from their loved ones, but we must help to overcome that, especially if they're to be here for days." Louise added a splash of cream to her coffee. "We need something that will keep them from brooding."

"I'll be happy to put everyone to work in here, but having too many cooks in the kitchen is never a good thing." Jane glanced at the bucket beside the back door in which Alice kept the greenery that she had used to make her wreath. "Alice, I like your idea about asking them to help us with the decorating. We still have a couple of boxes of things to unpack and we definitely need more ornaments for the tree."

"As long as we keep it low-key. Decorating might

remind them of home," Louise said. "I don't want to make them more homesick than they already are."

Jane sat back. "Unless you blow up their hometowns, Louie, I don't think that's going to happen."

Louise tapped a finger against her cheek. "Perhaps if we go about doing what we normally do, they will want to join in and help us."

"What if they don't?" Jane's smile dimmed.

"I don't know, Jane, but I think Louise is right. Maybe we should just do what we normally do for guests," Alice said. "We've always been able to make people feel right at home. Why should the holidays be any different?"

Jane pursed her lips. "Can we still pray for a van to show up, or would that be selfish and mean and unChristian?"

"We can pray for anything, and you do not have a single mean, selfish, unChristian bone in your body." Louise nodded toward the window. "At least the Good Lord is giving us a beautiful, white Christmas."

Jane suppressed a sigh. Christmas might look white for the moment, but if they did not find some way to cheer up their five guests, it was quickly going to turn a dismal shade of blue.

⁓

Coping with a full house was nothing new for the Howard sisters, except for the fact that Grace Chapel Inn's visitors were for the most part happy and satisfied people relaxing on vacation or taking time from a business trip while passing through the region.

The guests living under their roof at present were not happy people. They tried to put on a willing, cheerful demeanor, but when they discovered that a foot and a half of snow had fallen, and more was coming down every moment, their spirits drooped again.

"I never really believed in luck, good or bad," Edwina said as she picked at her breakfast, "but I'm beginning to think that this tour has been jinxed from the start."

Jane popped into the dining room to check on the guests and took a tray upstairs for Allan Hansford, who was still feeling too ill to leave his bed.

"All the major highways are closed?" Laura asked for a second time as Alice refilled her coffee. "*All* of them? You're sure that's what the report said?"

"I'll turn on the radio in the parlor if you'd like to listen to it after breakfast," Alice offered. "But people are already stranded all over the area."

Laura drummed her bright-red fingernails against the table top. "Last night I hired—at great expense to myself, I might add—a private car to come and pick me up and take me back to the city."

Max grunted. "Say good-bye to your deposit."

The rhythm of her tapping nails increased. "Can't we

call someone and tell them that it's an emergency? Have them plow the roads?"

For a moment Alice was so stupefied by the request that all she could do was stare at the younger woman.

"You can try," Max said. "People who have to work during the holidays can always use a good laugh."

"This isn't funny," Laura snapped.

Alice noticed that Edwina was also staring at the younger woman, but the look on her face did not reveal shock as much as it did disappointment.

"Were you going to mention this private car to anyone, Laura?" the schoolteacher asked.

The interior decorator gave her a sharp look, then her cheeks grew red. "I would have."

"If this storm is as bad as they say, we'll probably lose the power," Max said. "Where do you store your extra firewood, Alice?"

"We keep it in a bin in the shed at the side of the house," Alice told him. "I should have thought of that. We'll need to bring in as much as we can."

The businessman nodded. "Venson, you and I will go out after breakfast and deal with that."

Ted looked across the table at him. "We will?"

"You're not afraid of a little snow, are you?" When the younger man shook his head, Max smiled. "Good." He turned to Edwina and Laura. "You two can help Miss Howard and her sisters get things ready in here. Even with the fireplaces, we'll need extra blankets, flashlights and candles."

"I don't feel well." Laura pressed a palm to her head. "I should go lie down."

"Doing something will make you feel better." Max drained his coffee and rose. "Ted, if you're finished, let's get cracking."

With a look of near hero-worship, Ted nodded and followed the businessman out of the dining room.

Alice was about to release the breath she was holding when Laura abruptly got to her feet.

"Where is my bag?" she demanded loudly. Her face was very pale as she looked around her chair. "I had it right here."

"I didn't see you bring down a bag," Alice said. She saw Louise look in on them from the kitchen and gave her older sister a small shake of her head.

"It had my snow globe in it," she said, her voice growing more shrill. "I had to pay *thirty dollars* for that snow globe and now I won't even be able to give it to my client. She'll cancel her contract with me. She's a friend of my mother's. I have to have it. Where is it?" She started pacing around the room.

As Laura ranted about the snow globe, Edwina slipped out of the room. She returned just as Laura's voice was bordering on a shriek and held out the interior decorator's purse.

"Here," she said, putting the bag in her hands. "You left this in your room. Now sit down and stop acting like a hysterical child."

Laura stared at her, open-mouthed.

"Don't think I haven't tried to be patient with you. We all have. But you're a grown woman, Laura, and it's time you started behaving like one."

"How dare you say that to me! You don't know what I've been through. What I've sacrificed and suffered to build my business. My mother is going to be so angry that I failed, that I—" She pressed her napkin against her face and burst into tears.

"Oh, Laura." Edwina went over and sat next to the younger woman and put an arm around her narrow shoulders. "I'm sorry I spoke so harshly to you. This has been a terribly stressful time for all of us. You just need to let it out. There, there." She looked up at Alice and gave her a small nod, as if to let her know she would look after the distraught woman.

Alice left them alone and carried the dishes she had cleared into the kitchen, where Louise was washing up.

"Are you all right?" her older sister asked.

"Yes. Laura needed to vent a little frustration," Alice

told her. "Edwina is talking to her now. I think we should leave them alone for a bit."

Jane returned from upstairs. "I gave Allan the bad news and he took it well. He's feeling a little better, but I told him to stay in bed." She looked in the direction of the weeping coming from the dining room. "Do I hear the stone wall around Laura's heart finally giving way?"

"Max and Edwina said some things to her, and she's upset over the storm and her mother." Alice stacked the plates neatly in the dishwasher. "Evidently she hired a private-car service last night to come and pick her up, which won't happen now. More than anything else I think it embarrassed her to admit that."

Jane nodded. "A good cry will help."

The sisters worked together to tidy the kitchen and then discussed what needed to be prepared in the event of a possible power outage. Max and Ted made several trips outside to bring in firewood from the shed and then distributed it to the inn's fireplaces. Alice put out the extra blankets they might need, while Louise brought out the storm lamps, candles and flashlights. Jane put together the ingredients for several meals so that they could be made quickly and with minimum effort on the inn's gas stove.

The sounds of stomping on the rear porch announced their aunt's arrival just as Alice and Jane were regrouping in the kitchen. When she joined them powdered from the storm, she was too cold at first to do more than let her teeth chatter. Jane quickly warmed her up with a cup of hot, sweet ginger tea.

"If I were a bear, I'd go find a cave and stay there until spring," their aunt said once she was able to unclench her jaw. "It must be twenty below out there."

"Colder with the wind-chill factor." Jane used a hand towel to whisk the melting snowflakes from her aunt's short red hair. "You should have waited until the storm cleared a bit before coming over."

She waved a hand. "I faced worse when we were living on the farm. Besides, I have some news from town. If we're still snowed in by Christmas Eve, Pastor Thompson's made arrangements to have his sermon broadcast over one of the local AM radio stations in Riverton. He's going to call the station on the telephone and they're going to broadcast his call, just like they do with talk radio."

"What a clever idea." Alice said. "Here I had resigned myself to missing Christmas Eve service this year too."

"There's a blizzard burying us under tons of snow and you still found a way to get the latest gossip?" Jane teased. "You're more dedicated than the post office, Aunt Ethel."

"I should say so. Our mail carrier still takes a week to deliver my electric bill." Ethel touched her lips with her fingertips and frowned. "Do you have some lip balm, Jane? I'm getting a little chapped."

"I think I left some at the front desk. Be right back." Jane departed.

"Here, Alice. I found what you were looking for." Ethel immediately took a small, brown, paper-wrapped package from where it was tucked inside her jacket. "Now go on and hide it, quick, before Miss Nosy gets back."

Alice nearly ran into Louise as she hurried out of the kitchen. Her older sister greeted their aunt and glanced over her shoulder. "What sent Alice racing out of here?"

Ethel gave her a mysterious smile. "Just a little something for Christmas."

Chapter Eighteen

Sunday stretched out long, silent and then dark as the power failed in the afternoon. Ethel insisted on returning to the carriage house so that she could watch over her home during the bad weather, but she promised to return once the conditions cleared. The Howard sisters' five guests spent the day quietly, either resting in their candlelit rooms or sitting around the inn, pretending to read but mostly staring out of the windows at the storm.

Laura and Allan kept to their rooms, while Edwina sat in the parlor by a storm lamp and knitted a tiny, striped afghan for the grandchild she would not be able to see. Ted seemed to wander in and out of the rooms like a restless ghost, while Max silently watched over the fireplaces and kept them well-stocked with wood.

Louise had insisted that all three sisters give the visitors some time to adjust to the idea of being at Grace Chapel Inn for the holidays.

"We should just go about our normal daily routine while they acclimate to their situation," she told her sisters.

"I know they'll come around when it gets closer to Christmas."

Alice had volunteered to prepare lunch so that Louise and Jane could go to work on decorating the parlor. Unpacking the box of decorations made Louise quickly forget about their unhappy situation, as the contents included Madeleine Howard's collection of wooden Christmas toys, given to her by her parents each year in her stocking.

Louise smiled as she took out one of the old, wooden jumping jacks that their mother had treasured. "This was her favorite, remember? The purple one with the yellow hat."

"I loved making that jack jump." Jane's eyes got a far-away look in them. "I thought it was much more fun to play with than those silly Darcey dolls Santa kept leaving for me."

"You were doll-resistant," Louise agreed. "Of course, Darcey couldn't do jumping jacks."

"Sure she could," Jane said, giving her a slow smile. "With a little wire and some fine tuning of her limbs, which popped right out of the joint sockets, by the way."

"I don't think I want to hear any more," Louise said, noticing that Edwina had stopped knitting and was listening to their conversation.

"You were always a soft touch for dolls, big sister."

"While you were like a wild child with them." She sighed. "I was too old to have a Darcey doll when they came out, but I would have liked one when I was a girl. I was very fond of the Darceys I bought for you and Cynthia."

Her youngest sister laughed. "Then I shouldn't tell you about when and where I took Darcey deep-sea diving."

"Deep-Sea-Diving Darcey?" A chuckle escaped Edwina. "I don't remember that version."

"Well, there actually wasn't an official deep-sea-diving version. I put Luau-Lovely Darcey through extensive marine training." Jane's eyes sparkled. "Guess what I used for a pool."

"I don't think you want to hear this, Edwina," Louise warned. "She was the kind of child who could make the straightest hair curl."

"You had Darcey dolls, didn't you, Edwina?" When she nodded, Jane asked, "Didn't you take them on adventures?"

"What she means is, did you scalp them, drown them or try to send them to the moon on a rocket launcher?" Louise translated.

"It was not a rocket launcher," Jane said. "It was a firecracker."

"Which I can verify does not make Darcey fly when you strap it to her back and light it," Louise added. "We had a very nice memorial service for her, however."

Now the schoolteacher laughed. "You must have been a handful, Jane. I'm afraid I was not quite as adventurous myself." She looked down at the little afghan that she was making. "You know, I learned to knit so that I could make clothes for my Darceys. My Aunt Margaret taught me one winter when she was staying with us."

"You do knit beautifully." Jane paused to admire her work. "Louise tried to teach me, but the yarn kept snarling into knots."

"No, you *tied* it into knots, as I recall," Louise said. "That was the year you wanted to become a pirate, or maybe it was the year you wanted to be a cowgirl and herd cattle at a ranch in Montana. I can't remember which."

Jane dug into the box and took out a red stocking, which had several large holes in it. "Oh rats! Or, more likely, *moths*. I wanted to hang them up this year, like we did when we were girls. Just for decoration."

"Let me see." Edwina came over to examine the damage. "You could patch them, but they wouldn't look the same."

"It's okay." Jane shrugged. "It was a silly idea anyway."

"I don't think it was. My parents always made a fuss about preparing our stockings." Edwina sighed. "I miss that —waking up Christmas morning and hurrying to see what Santa had left in my stocking. It was so exciting, pulling one thing after another out of it until I reached the toe. The best gift was always at the very bottom."

"I have some yarn," Louise said, sounding thoughtful. "Maybe I could knit up a few stockings before Christmas."

"With all we have to do around here?" Jane shook her head. "It's not that important."

"Yes, it is," Edwina insisted. "I could make a few, if I could borrow some yarn. I don't have any Christmas colors with me."

"I have my knitting bag in the study, right next to the brown armchair." Louise smiled. "Please, help yourself to whatever you like."

"I'll go look at it now. I've never made a stocking pattern before, but it shouldn't be that hard. I could make one for everyone." Edwina hesitated. "Would you have some little things we could put in them as gifts for the others? I'll pay for them."

Jane nodded. "We'd be happy to provide them. We can't have empty stockings on Christmas morning. Perhaps we'll talk about paying at another time."

"That would be wonderful." Beaming, Edwina departed for the study.

"You know, that is the happiest I have seen her since the group came here." Louise looked down at the box of decorations. "What did Ted love about Christmas as a child, I wonder."

"I don't know," Jane admitted. A slow smile appeared on her face. "But we're going to find out, aren't we?"

"I think a little reminiscing about childhood could be just the thing. Remember how much everyone enjoyed talking about their favorite family recipes for the holidays over dinner last night? Our guests will not mind if we ask them to contribute something to our decorations or holiday preparations by recreating one of their favorite Christmas memories." Louise tapped a finger against her cheek. "Those memories never make us sad. They are part of the magic of Christmas."

"Very sneaky, big sister," Jane said, "As long as no one has a treasured childhood memory of building a ten-foot, red-and-green Tyrannosaurus Rex and having it attack the tree."

"I'll check with Ted, but I think we are safe from that." She frowned. "Do you think it will work? Reminding them of their childhood Christmases?"

Edwina hurried back into the parlor. "Do you have Miss Reed's phone number?" she asked. "If I could call her, I'm sure she'd be willing to share her stocking pattern with me. I can simply enlarge it to make the stockings people-sized instead of cat-sized."

"That would work," Jane said and gave her older sister a big smile.

⁓

Alice had doubted Louise's idea at first, but seeing how happy Edwina was as she began knitting stockings for everyone had convinced her to give it a try. When she had gone up to check on Allan, who was still quite miserable, she had told him the story about Jane's buying the gingerbread men for the children at the bakery in town and mentioned her own favorite childhood memory of decorating sugar cookies with her father.

"My mother would make a big gingerbread house every year," Allan told her. My brother and I always helped her decorate them with cookies and candy when we were little, but as we got older she would bake the gingerbread and let us design and build the houses ourselves."

"Is this tradition responsible for your love of architecture?" Alice asked. "Or were you just interested in snitching bits of the building materials?"

Allan laughed. "Both, I believe."

"I do love gingerbread houses, but I've never made one," Alice said. "Our father was not much of a baker."

"They're not difficult at all. The trick is to make the sheets of gingerbread very thin, and cut the pieces out while the gingerbread is still warm and soft from the oven. The recipes for the gingerbread and the white icing that acts like plaster for it are in any standard cookbook." He sat up and reached for his sketchpad. "I could draw up what pieces you need to cut out of the gingerbread. There's one I made when I was a teenager that looked like a real log cabin."

In view of Alice's success with Allan, Jane had decided to try Louise's idea with Laura, who emerged from her room the next morning looking wan and asking if the sisters had any aspirin. When she returned with some from her room, Jane mentioned Allan's idea about the gingerbread house and also hinted that making candy might be a good idea.

Laura seemed momentarily lost in thought. "My grandmother was from Maine and she hated store-bought candy. She said the chemical dyes in it always made them taste bitter."

"She never let you have candy?" Jane asked, surprised.

"Not anything you could buy at a store. She made candy for me out of maple syrup and snow." Laura's thin lips uncrimped a little. "If you have some pure maple syrup and a candy thermometer, I think I could make a soft version of it."

"What's the snow for?" Jane asked.

"To cool it and make it harden. You boil the syrup until it reaches a certain temperature and then you pour it on snow." She gestured with her hands. "We would make big pans of it and fight over the best pieces. We ate sour pickles in between." She saw the look Jane gave her. "You can't eat maple sugar candy without breaking it up with something sour. It's a tradition."

Sour pickles and maple candy? "I'd love to try it. Why not use today to plan your candy production. I'll guarantee you kitchen time tomorrow for your specialty." Jane hoped that she had enough antacid on hand for the upset stomachs that combination would produce.

Ted had already gotten involved in Allan's gingerbread house project before Alice or Jane could ask him about his favorite childhood memory, which left Max. Alice decided to ask him that night after dinner, when they were clearing the table.

"Waffles," he said at once.

"What sort of waffles?"

"Any kind my mother made. She had about a hundred different variations, but on Christmas morning she always made real Belgian waffles. She would let me pour the batter over the waffle iron and watch it to make sure it wouldn't burn. I taught my wife that recipe when we got married." He cleared his throat and murmured something else.

"I'm sorry, what did you say?"

"My favorite kind when I was a boy were when Mother made waffle men," Max said, and two flags of red color appeared on his cheekbones. "If you pour the batter a certain way, you can make waffles shaped like people. I used to put blueberries in the batter to make faces for them."

"Would you make some of the waffle men for us tomorrow morning?" Alice asked. "I know I'd love to try them."

Max nodded. "If you've got a waffle iron, I can make you a whole army of them."

The storm clouds slowly dwindled until they finally cleared on Tuesday at dawn. They left behind a porcelain blue sky and five-foot drifts of dense, alabaster snow. When Alice walked out onto the front porch, it seemed as if the world had been wrapped in white mink, sprinkled with diamond dust and presented as a gift of dazzling perfection.

The stirring up of childhood memories over the past couple of days had affected their guests even more than Louise had expected. Some of the excitement of being a child at Christmas returned as they sought to recapture something that had mattered to them years before. As a result, the five people staying at Grace Chapel Inn had undergone rather amazing transformations.

Alice found it heartwarming as well that each of the memories connected their guests to something they had shared with and learned from a beloved family member: Edwina's aunt teaching her to knit, Laura's grandmother making homemade candy, Allan's mother building ginger-bread houses.

It wasn't surprising, however. Alice knew that it was family who made the holidays special, and she treasured how her father and sisters had created many wonderful memories for her. *I only hope that I can do the same for my sisters.*

"Good morning, Alice," Edwina said as she came downstairs carrying her knitting bag. "I almost have the last one finished." She held up two long needles, and the red-and-white striped stocking attached to them. "Thanks to Louise for her gift of yarn, we'll be able to hang up one for everyone by Christmas Eve."

"I wish Viola could see these." Alice admired her neat handiwork. "Do you think you could make one for Wendell?"

"I already have." The schoolteacher reached into her bag and pulled out a smaller version of the stocking, this one with a white mouse worked into the red stitching. "Miss Reed made me promise that I would when she gave me the pattern over the phone."

The two women walked into the dining room, where Ted Venson was having breakfast with Allan Hansford. Both men were discussing the house plans Allan had drawn on a sheet of paper between them on the table, but they paused to greet Alice and Edwina.

"How are you doing with the building plans?" Edwina asked, peering over Ted's shoulder at the design. "Oh my. Should you apply to the zoning commission before you build that?"

"No, but we are rethinking the hot tub and the guest cottage out back," Allan teased back.

"We've got all of our materials together," Ted told her. "As soon as we're finished with the breakfast dishes we're going to start construction."

The schoolteacher laughed. "We'll have to look for some Lincoln Logs next."

Alice studied the older man's face. "Are you feeling up to doing this, Allan?"

"I haven't had so much as a sniffle since last night." He looked over as Jane came out of the kitchen carrying a tray. "Now if I can just tear myself away from these Belgian waffles."

"You men ate all the Belgian ones. These are blueberry," her younger sister told him as she placed a new stack of golden-brown waffles on the table. She paused for a moment to pick up the empty juice pitcher. "We have a new pot of coffee brewing, but the teapot on the table is full." She went back into the kitchen.

Alice left Edwina at the table and went in to see if Jane needed any help, only to find her talking to Max, who was scowling at the stove.

"It hates me." He showed her a slightly too-brown waffle. "See?"

"It's a gas stove, Max. You just have to get used to it." Jane reached down and lowered the flame a fraction. "You're doing great."

"I'm scorching things."

"You are not. Besides, we can use the extra crispy ones for dessert tonight." She looked over at Alice. "Did you see Laura? She was going outside to get some snow."

"She must have gone out back." Alice looked over as the kitchen door opened and the interior decorator came in carrying two tin pie plates filled with white, fluffy snow. "Here she is."

"This had better be as good as I remember it," Laura said as she put aside the pans in order to slip out of her coat and mittens. "I think my ears have turned to ice." She glared at Max. "Have you been watching the candy thermometer, like I told you to?"

"Yes, and it's distracting from my waffles."

"Move aside, you big old grouch." Laura casually nudged him aside and peered at the glass thermometer clipped to the side of a pot filled with a brown, bubbling mixture. "There, that's perfect." She used a pot holder to remove the pan from the stove and brought it over to the two pie plates of snow. "Now, if I can just do it the way Grandmother did."

Laura carefully poured the mixture over the snow in thin scrolls, which instantly solidified and turned a pale brown.

"So far, so good," Jane said, peering at the pans.

Laura set the pan aside. "I still have to test it." She took a toothpick and gently prodded the mixture. "That's it. We have real maple sugar candy." She began transferring the scrolls from the pans onto wax paper.

Alice congratulated her, and Jane gave her a one-armed

hug. Max reached for a piece of the candy, only to earn a tap on the back of his hand from Laura.

"No candy for breakfast," she said and gave him another nudge. "Go sit down and eat. I'll finish the rest of the waffles."

"I can do that, Laura," Jane said. "Go have a cup of tea and check out Allan's house plan. He and Ted are ready to start putting it together."

"Yes, and if we don't watch them, they might build a replica of Philadelphia's city hall, complete with William Penn's statue on top," Alice warned, making everyone chuckle.

Alice waited until their guests had returned to the dining room before she released the laugh she had been holding. "Extra-crispy waffles for dessert?"

"With a liberal amount of ice cream, strategically applied." Her younger sister grinned. "They hold up better."

"I can't believe how well this is working out." Alice shook her head and sat down for a moment at the little kitchen table. "I certainly never expected to see Max cooking or Laura making candy."

"There's a kid inside everyone," Jane reminded her. "Convincing them to let their inner child come out and play was a stroke of genius."

Chapter Nineteen

espite the lack of electricity, buoyant spirits prevailed through Christmas Eve morning, as everyone pitched in to add something special to the holiday preparations. Snow fell, not as it had before, but prettily over Acorn Hill.

Allan and Ted unveiled the gingerbread house at breakfast by placing it as the centerpiece for the table. Two miniature stories of rich, dark gingerbread, exactly cut and assembled to look like Viola Reed's Queen Anne home, rose from drifts of white-icing snow. Cookies, candies and pretzels formed the trim and house details. The crowning touch was the foil-wrapped chocolate Santa Claus going down the sugar wafer chimney.

Edwina's ten knitted stockings—one for each guest, each of the Howards, their aunt and a small one for Wendell—hung waiting on the mantel in the parlor. She had personalized each with different combinations of stitches and yarns. She had even embroidered a set of initials on the cuff of each one to identify its owner.

Laura had made enough maple-sugar candy for everyone, and after being encouraged by Jane, tried recreating some of her grandmother's other homemade candies. She also showed Max how adding a bit of maple sugar to his coffee gave it a rich, mellow sweetness that, in her opinion, ordinary table sugar could not provide. Beaming, she promised everyone a surprise for Christmas Eve dinner.

The guests also insisted on taking turns in the kitchen with preparing meals, which allowed Louise, Alice and Jane time to finish working on their own gifts for their guests, along with the treats that Edwina had suggested.

"We can't have them wake up to empty stockings on Christmas morning," Louise had said. "Not after all they have done to contribute to our holiday."

Since the deep snow had kept the Howard sisters from going shopping, they decided to follow their guests' examples and make do with homemade gifts. Jane had packed five pretty boxes with her fancy angelight cookies, and tagged them with cards listing the recipes for a dish she had made that each guest had particularly enjoyed.

Alice had taken pint-sized plastic berry baskets and filled them with an assortment of tea bags and flavored instant coffee packets. Over the years she and her father had amassed a large collection of holiday coffee mugs, and she picked five of her most cheerful for the baskets.

Louise had used old sheet music to wrap five picture frames, which she had also personalized for each guest with his or her family name written down one side of the frame in fine calligraphy, using metallic-gold ink. She had also made up five small packets of photos from those she had taken of Grace Chapel Inn and the sights of Acorn Hill. She had intended to send many of the pictures to Cynthia, but she could make more from the negatives after the holidays.

I will have to convince my daughter to take some time off from that hectic job of hers to come for a visit soon, Louise thought as she put away the negatives in her room. She missed Cynthia most acutely during the holidays, which unfortunately were always a busy time for her daughter's publishing company. Still, she had her sisters and her memories. *I should tell the guests about the Christmas when Cynthia gave Eliot her chicken pox.*

It was Jane, and the memory of Cynthia's unfortunately timed bout with chicken pox, that made Louise recall another photograph, one she hadn't thought of in years.

Did I save it? She had tried not to think about that time very often, but enough years had passed now that she felt a pang of longing to see the photo again.

Louise went to her closet and took down the box in which she kept her old school memorabilia and sorted through it until she found her first photo album. She sat down on the bed with it and began looking through the pages, smiling at the youthful photos of herself. At last she came to the section that she had made from the time when she was a sophomore in high school.

That had been a terrible year for the Howards. Her mother Madeleine had passed away after Jane's birth, and Daniel had had to cope with shattering grief and a new baby all at once. Louise always remembered the Christmas of that year, which might have been the saddest of her life.

On one page Louise had written a Bible verse, Ecclesiastes 7:14, which a friend of her mother's had read at Madeleine's memorial service: "When times are good, be happy; but when times are bad, consider: God has made the one as well as the other."

That verse had perplexed her for weeks after her mother's death, until Jane had started to change from a helpless newborn into a very active infant. It had been that change that had drawn Louise out of her grief more than anything else, for seeing Jane's bright eyes and happy smile, and hearing her sweet laughter and cooing gurgles had made it impossible to be sad.

I wonder if you will ever know how much you meant to us, she thought as she gazed at one photo in particular. *You were like a gift from God, sent to remind us that even in death, there is life.*

"Louise?" Alice was standing outside her open door.

Feeling too emotional to speak, Louise gestured for her sister to come in and carefully removed the photograph from the paper tabs at the corners. Without a word she handed it to her sister.

For a long moment Alice simply looked at the photo

too. Then she gave Louise a beautiful smile. "I completely forgot about this. Has Jane ever seen it?"

"I don't think I ever showed it to her." Louise gazed up at her middle sister. "I want to frame it and give it as my Christmas gift for her, Alice. What do you think?"

Alice gave her older sister a hug. "It's perfect."

During a break in the weather, a snowy Ethel Buckley arrived for afternoon tea. Once she had brushed off and warmed up, she slipped out of the kitchen and brought a cardboard box into the reception area, where Alice was doing some last-minute gift wrapping.

"Jane said you were in here." She looked at the berry boxes, which Alice had wrapped up in tulle and topped with raffia-straw bows. "That has such a nice country look to it."

Alice grinned and then sniffed the air. "Do I smell peaches?"

"You do. I've been doing a little baking." Ethel set the box down on the desk and opened it. "Thank goodness for gas stoves. Have you heard when the power might be restored?"

"Tonight, if we're lucky. Oh, how cute." Alice admired the little beaded angel ornaments her aunt had produced.

"Carol Matthews showed us how to make these at my last craft exchange." Ethel placed six of them on the desk. "There's one for your tree and one for each of your guests."

"We'll put them in the stockings tonight." Alice peered into the box, which held several dozen of her aunt's blue-ribbon-winning peach tarts, wrapped up in neat bundles with colorful cellophane. "Do I get some of those tarts?"

"If you've been a good girl, yes," Ethel said. "I made up a few for you and your sisters, and some for your guests too."

Alice was touched. "You didn't have to do that."

"Nonsense. Kept me busy during the storm." Ethel made a shooing gesture. "I had planned on making them for Lloyd—you know how much he loves them—but I can always whip up another batch after he shakes his flu bug."

"Thank you, Aunt. I know they'll enjoy them." Alice checked her watch. "You're staying for dinner, aren't you? Pastor Thompson will be giving his Christmas sermon at seven tonight. I thought we would gather everyone together in Father's study after dinner to listen to it." She made a mental note to check the batteries in the radio, in the event that the power was not restored.

Ethel chuckled softly. "I haven't spent an evening listening to the radio since I was a girl." The sound of laughter made her turn her head and glance back through the door. "Things are a lot more cheerful around here. You'd have never known it a few days ago."

"Ted and Allan have everyone in the dining room working on decorating gingerbread men." Alice smiled. "Laura insisted they make some of them gingerbread women."

Ethel's eyebrows rose. "Aren't they a bit old for that?"

"I hope not. I want to make a couple of gingerbread inn-keepers myself." Alice picked up the box. "Let's put these in the kitchen."

Just then, however, the phone rang. Alice picked up the receiver. "Happy Holidays from Grace Chapel Inn, Alice Howard speaking, may I help you?"

"I need to speak to Jane Howard," an unfamiliar man's voice said.

At the same time, there was a click on the line. "I've got it, Alice," Jane said over the kitchen extension. "Thanks."

"Okay." Alice hung up the phone and gave it a quizzical look. The man did not sound like anyone she knew.

"Who was that?"

"I don't know. Someone asking for Jane."

⌒

Jane waited until she heard a click on the other end before she spoke again. "I'm so glad you called. I was afraid you had gotten stranded somewhere."

"I was, for a time. I'm trying to find a way out there." The man's voice hesitated. "If you think I'm still welcome."

"Of course you are." She smiled as Louise walked in. "Is there anything you need me to do? Should I say something?"

"No. If I can't make it, then . . ." he cleared his throat. "I'll try another time."

"All right. Call me and let me know. I'll talk to you soon." Jane hung up the phone. "Did you all run out of candy?"

"Not yet, but Allan wants some powdered sugar for the shrubbery." Louise glanced at the telephone. "Who was that who called?"

"Just a friend." Jane didn't want to spoil her biggest surprise for Christmas.

"I was hoping that the power would be restored by now." Her older sister brought out a box of 4-X sugar from the pantry and hesitated, as if she were making up her mind about something. "Jane, you don't feel overwhelmed by all that's going on in your kitchen, do you?"

That startled her a little. "No. Why would you think that?"

Louise set the box on the counter. "It is just that you seem to be contributing so much to your guests—and to your sisters."

"You really worry about me too much, big sister. I'm fine and nothing is going to ruin our Christmas." She made a face. "That already hasn't happened, I mean."

"We're together." Louise came over and took hold of her hands. "That is the only gift that I wanted."

She smiled. "Me too."

Jane had wanted to make Christmas Eve dinner a cooperative effort, carrying over the idea of sharing with each other the happy memories of their childhood.

Six cooks were five too many for her kitchen, however, so she had everyone take turns that afternoon preparing a side dish to go with the baked capons that she had planned for the evening meal.

Laura was the last to work on her contribution to dinner. "Do you think everyone will like this?"

Jane grinned as she opened the oven door to check the capons. "No one ever minds having *two* desserts."

"My grandfather never did," Laura said. She smiled a little. "He had a horrendous sweet tooth. I think that's why Grandma loved to make candy and kept big jars of it in her kitchen year-round."

"Did you ever visit them in Maine?"

Laura shook her head. "Not very often. My mother couldn't stand the farm. She left home after school and never wanted to go back. As I got older, the only time I saw my grandparents was when they came to visit us. Grandma made the trip every year, and when Grandpa got too old to handle the long drive, they would come down on the bus."

"Did your mother have the resources to visit them for the holidays?"

A humorless laugh escaped her. "My mother married very well, several times, and always had more than enough money. We had a housekeeper and a cook, and I had a nanny. Even so, whenever Grandma would visit, she would insist on making Christmas dinner herself."

"It sounds like they loved you a lot."

The younger woman shrugged. "They probably came to see me just to spite my mother. I think they knew she was ashamed of them." She looked down into the mixing bowl. "I never was, though—no matter what Mother said about them. They were married for fifty-three years. Can you imagine, being with the same man for that long?"

"If he was the right man, yes."

"Well, I've never found a man like that." Laura's voice changed. "My grandmother spent her whole life with him. After Grandpa passed away, she came down on the bus for one last visit. She went home and died alone a few weeks later."

Jane felt her heart constrict. "That must have been so hard for you."

Laura shook her head. "I was glad she went to be with him. I was just a kid, but somehow I knew that she couldn't live without him."

But you felt abandoned, Jane thought, *because she was more of a mother to you than the woman who gave birth to you.* All at once she felt as if she understood what drove Laura a little better.

"We lost our father recently," she told the younger woman. "Whenever I feel sad, I try to think of him being reunited with our mother."

"I don't know why it still bothers me." She stared blindly at the window. "Grandma never had a job, never left the farm except to see me and never spent a day away from my grandfather. The only time I ever saw her without him was that last visit."

"Being a devoted wife is nothing to be ashamed of."

"Not according to my mother," Laura said bitterly. "She always said that men are only good for one thing—alimony. She's the reason I've never gotten married." She made a disgusted sound. "And now I've become just like her. Cold, obsessed with money, and indifferent to anyone's feelings but my own."

"You don't have to be like her," Jane said. "You can be whoever you want to be."

"I wanted to be like my grandmother. My mother thought her parents' life was contemptible because they didn't have much money or a fancy house." Laura suddenly thumped down the spoon in her hand. "She was wrong. My grandmother didn't need those things. She was the happiest woman in the world."

"Everyone should do what makes her happy," Jane said. "Not what someone else expects. But it's hard to find the courage to do that." She had certainly struggled with it herself.

"Maybe it's just easier to go along with what your parents and your friends expect of you." The younger woman grabbed a paper towel and wiped up the spill she'd made. "But my grandmother never did anything the easy way."

"I guess you have to look at the results and decide if they were worth it." Jane picked up the glass jar of maple candy that Laura had made and took it over to set it on the counter beside her. "Like this candy she taught you to make. It's not fancy and you'd never find it in a store."

"But it's made with love." Laura touched the jar. "You can't buy what comes from the heart."

Phone calls from the guests' family members began coming in just before dinner, but this time the conversations were much happier. The five guests kept them brief, too, so that all would have a chance to use the phone and wish their loved ones a Merry Christmas.

Jane had brought out Madeleine's good china, since they always used it for holiday dinners, and drafted Max to help her with serving the different dishes everyone had made.

Louise had everyone join hands and she said the blessing. "Father in heaven, we thank You for this wonderful meal and the hands that helped to make it. Your blessings have brought new friends to our home and new joy to our hearts. Guide us forever with the light of Your word and the love of Your spirit, through Christ our Lord. Amen."

Jane's savory capons came out delightfully tender and Edwina's twice-baked sweet potatoes, topped with ground pecans and a touch of nutmeg, and Ted's vegetable platter looked wonderful.

Ted refused to take full credit for his colorful contribution, however. "If it wasn't for Jane and her skill with a garnish knife," he said, gesturing toward the raw vegetables cut into frills, flowers and other fanciful shapes, "I might have chopped everything into sticks."

Allan made everyone laugh by explaining his reasons for making the pitcher of minted iced tea. "My wife has forbidden me to do anything in the kitchen but boil water, and only then with direct supervision," he told the group. "I think it was the fifth pot I scorched that made the kitchen permanently out of bounds for me."

After dinner, Jane urged Max to remain seated while she brought out his leftover waffles, which she had steamed and rolled around vanilla ice cream speckled with maraschino cherries.

"You've done enough for one night." She turned to the interior decorator. "Would you mind bringing in your dish, Laura?"

Laura looked slightly embarrassed as she carried in the dessert she had made, and everyone around the table stared at the tower of orange-glazed baked puffs, stacked together to form a Christmas tree and draped with a web of delicate strands of spun sugar and stars cut from fresh citrus slices.

"This is a Maine orange tree," she told them. "At least, that's what my grandmother called it."

"That is the most gorgeous thing I have ever seen," Edwina breathed.

"I always liked it when I was a little girl," the interior decorator said simply as she set the platter in the center of the table. She couldn't hide her flush of pleasure, though, and the look she gave Jane spoke volumes.

After dessert the sisters, along with Ethel and their guests, gathered in Daniel Howard's study to listen to Pastor Thompson's Christmas Eve radio sermon.

"I wish the celebration at Grace Chapel hadn't been canceled," Alice said as she sat down beside Louise. "We have a candlelight service every year and the choir sings so beautifully."

"We spent all that time decorating the church this year too," her aunt said, looking faintly disgruntled.

"Yes, but we're warm, happy and surrounded by friends," Jane said as she went over to tune in the station. "This is the next best thing to being there."

After playing several Christmas carols, the radio announcer came on and introduced Rev. Thompson.

"Good evening, friends." Although he was being relayed by telephone, the pastor's voice came over the radio clearly, as if he were standing at the radio station and speaking into the microphone. "The recent bad weather has made it impossible for us to be together in the flesh, but that is not an unusual thing for Christians. Throughout history, we have had to carry our faith with us, wherever we go and whenever we are separated from those we love. You could say that by now, we're almost used to it."

"He sounds wonderful," Ethel whispered. "Just like a professional."

"Tonight, Christians all over the world are celebrating the most holy night of the year. We come together on this night to worship and pray, and to thank Almighty God for the gift that He made to the world, the gift of Jesus Christ, our Savior. We come together now, in spirit, to offer up our love and our gratitude to God, for bringing the light of salvation into the world through Jesus Christ.

"We all know the story and yet we never tire of hearing it. I'd like to tell you the story again, from the book of Luke, chapter two 'In those days Caesar Augustus issued a decree that a census should be taken of the entire Roman world. (This was the first census that took place while Quirinius was governor of Syria.) And everyone went to his own town to register.

"'So Joseph also went up from the town of Nazareth in Galilee to Judea, to Bethlehem the town of David, because he belonged to the house and line of David. He went there to register with Mary, who was pledged to be married to him and was expecting a child. While they were there, the time came for the baby to be born, and she gave birth to her first-born, a son. She wrapped him in cloths and placed him in a manger, because there was no room for them in the inn.'"

Max rose unexpectedly and left the room.

"'And there were shepherds living out in the fields nearby, keeping watch over their flocks at night. An angel of the Lord appeared to them, and the glory of the Lord shone around them, and they were terrified. But the angel said to them, "Do not be afraid. I bring you good news of great joy that will be for all the people. Today in the town of David a Savior has been born to you; he is Christ the Lord. This will be a sign to you: You will find a baby wrapped in cloths and lying in a manger."'"

Louise, who was sitting beside Jane, put her arm around her youngest sister.

"'Suddenly a great company of the heavenly host appeared with the angel, praising God and saying, "Glory to God in the highest, and on earth peace to men on whom his favor rests."

"'When the angels had left them and gone into heaven, the shepherds said to one another, "Let's go to Bethlehem and see this thing that has happened, which the Lord has told us about." So they hurried off and found Mary and

Joseph, and the baby, who was lying in the manger. When they had seen him, they spread the word concerning what had been told them about this child, and all who heard it were amazed at what the shepherds said to them.

"'But Mary treasured up all these things and pondered them in her heart. The shepherds returned, glorifying and praising God for all the things they had heard and seen, which were just as they had been told.'"

Alice blinked back the tears that hearing the beloved Bible verses always brought to her eyes.

"Those words speak of a birth that happened two thousand years ago," Rev. Thompson said. "It was a supreme moment, a moment when the greatest love of all time was shown to mankind. My dear friends, as Christmas is upon us, let us tell this story to our families and our children and our friends. Tell them of what happened on this night, so very long ago in the town of Bethlehem. A town whose very name means 'the House of Bread.' Jesus would later say of Himself, 'I am the bread of life. He who comes to me will never go hungry, and he who believes in me will never be thirsty' [John 6:35].

"We are accustomed to going out during this season to share our joy with others. But joy is not simply the consequence of celebrations and gift-giving. Joy comes from Almighty God, the source of all happiness. When you feel joy, the light of heaven is illuminating your heart.

"For the many who have been separated by circum-
stance from their loved ones, I pray that you will look in
your heart for joy. The love of God makes all things simple,
and transforms our pain into peace. If not for the coming
of Jesus Christ, we might never have known how much love
God has for us, His children. We truly would have been left
alone and cold and hungry. Let us pray together now."

Jane bowed her head, but just before she closed her
eyes, she saw Max slip silently back into the room.

"Dear Father in heaven, You have filled our lives with
countless blessings, and our hearts with peace and love. We
thank You for this wonderful season and for the gifts it brings
to us, but most importantly, we thank You for the birth of
Your Son, Jesus Christ, who was Your gift to the world. Help
us to follow His teachings and find our way through the darkness. Give us the strength to find joy wherever we are, safe in
the knowledge that we are loved by You. Remind us that no
matter where we are, that we are never, ever alone. Through
the glory that is Jesus Christ Our Lord. Amen."

"Amen," echoed around the room.

Alice looked over to see Max surreptitiously wipe his
eyes, and she closed her own in a moment of private entreaty.
*Please, Lord, bring joy back into this man's life. Show him the path of peace
and help him reconcile with his son. That is the only gift I want this year.*

Louise ushered everyone into the parlor, where she played classic Christmas carols on the piano for their guests. Alice and Jane brought out eggnog and cookies, and encouraged the guests to sing.

"You don't want *me* to," Jane warned them. "The good crystal might not survive the experience."

Laura and Edwina were coerced into singing a duet of "Walking in a Winter Wonderland," which they performed beautifully: Laura had a surprisingly sweet soprano voice, which harmonized wonderfully with Edwina's contralto.

Ted obliged the group with a brief and rather comical rendition of "Deck the Halls," as he could not remember all the words and had to be prompted. That was followed by Allan, who got them all singing "The Twelve Days of Christmas."

Max walked up to the piano when they reached day twelve and asked Louise something in a low voice. She nodded, and after she finished the last verse Max stood next to the piano.

Alice noticed that he was scowling again and for a moment feared that the fact that he had received no phone calls had made him revert back to his former, melancholy detachment.

"I haven't done this in ten years or better," he told them in a very gruff voice. "But this song was my wife's favorite Christmas carol, and I would like to sing it in her memory."

Max then sang "Silent Night" in his deep baritone. Everyone grew still as they listened to the solemn carol, which was performed carefully and with great affection.

> Silent night, holy night,
> Son of God, love's pure light;
> Radiant beams from Thy holy face
> With the dawn of redeeming grace,
> Jesus Lord, at Thy birth
> Jesus Lord, at Thy birth.

Alice sighed as the deep emotion in the man's voice seemed to vibrate in her bones. It was the perfect ending to the evening.

Since it was growing late, Jane walked Ethel back to the carriage house, while Alice and Edwina tidied up the parlor. When she returned, the mantel clock struck midnight and everyone exchanged heartfelt wishes for a Merry Christmas before retiring for the evening.

It had been a lovely Christmas Eve, Alice decided as she went out to turn down the lamps in the front of the house. She was surprised to see Aunt Ethel's Christmas candle glowing on a table that had been set by one of the front windows, sending out the aroma of peppermint.

Max came out of the kitchen and noticed her standing by the window.

"I put that there a little earlier," he told her. "My wife

would always keep a candle in the window on Christmas Eve."

"I meant to do that myself, but I forgot about it." She looked out into the darkness. "It's so cold. I hope there is no one out there traveling tonight."

"There is," Max told her, "but I think Jesus Christ knows His way around."

Chapter Twenty

*J*ane woke up to electric light on Christmas morning and saw that it came from the lamp beside her bed; she had not turned it off before the power failed.

She scrambled out from under the covers. "We've got power." The floor was warm under her bare feet, thanks to the central heating.

Swiftly she dressed and hurried downstairs to see the Christmas tree lit up and brightly wrapped gifts piled around the base. The gift tags all listed three names: hers, Alice's and Louise's.

She looked around. "Did Santa actually make it through the snow drifts?" She still had hope that one special visitor would.

A yawning Edwina joined her at the foot of the stairs. "It would appear one of his helpers did." Her drowsy eyes glowed with happiness. "Merry Christmas, Jane."

"Merry Christmas to you too." Jane gave her an affectionate hug. "Should we wake up the whole house or go make coffee?"

"Coffee first," the schoolteacher said. "I especially don't want to make Max wait for his first cup. He's being too nice and I don't want to ruin it."

By the time Jane had the coffee brewing and the teakettle filled, her sisters and the rest of their guests had come downstairs. Edwina brought the filled stockings in from the parlor and handed them around, while Alice and Louise surveyed, with some bewilderment, the gifts left under the tree for them.

"You didn't go to all this trouble, did you?" Alice asked her older sister, who shook her head. "Then, who? Jane?"

"No, I believe that Jane used silver wrapping paper." Louise nodded toward two gifts sitting to one side, and scanned the smiling faces around them. "I have five more ideas about who it could have been, however."

Once everyone had a cup of coffee or tea, Edwina insisted that the sisters open their gifts first.

"You've put us before yourselves all week. Now it's your turn." She glanced at Ted, who had his camera ready.

Louise opened the first gift, which was rectangular and flat. Inside was a large framed drawing of Grace Chapel Inn, so precisely detailed that it showed even the wood grain on the siding.

It was signed by the artist, Allan Hansford.

"I had Ted smuggle some of your brochures up to me

while I was stuck in bed," the retired architect explained. "The photo of the inn on the cover gave me the basic exterior structure. After my allergies died down, I slipped outside a few times to get the detailing." He tapped the frame. "I stole this from my room. The nice little watercolor which was in it is safely stowed in the top of my closet."

"It is just beautiful," Louise said, touched by the talent and time that had gone into making the gift. "Thank you so much."

Alice opened the next gift, which contained three gorgeous scarves knitted in an airy pattern from blue, green and violet yarn, the same yarn Edwina had been using to make the little afghan for her grandchild.

"The blue is for Louise, the green for Alice and the purple for Jane," the smiling schoolteacher told them. "I have one for your aunt too."

"But what about your afghan?" Alice asked.

"What afghan? I unraveled it Sunday night." Edwina laughed. "Don't worry, I will make another. In fact, that poor child will receive enough things knitted by me to last her two lifetimes."

Jane opened Laura's gift, which was the antique snow globe with the three children carolers that the interior decorator had made such a fuss over buying. "Oh, Laura!"

"I never liked that client very much anyway," the interior

decorator said in a mock snooty voice before her expression softened. "It belongs in a house like this, with people like you."

Ted's gift was a collage of photos he had taken of Acorn Hill on his first day in town.

"It was the only roll of film I was able to have developed before we were stranded," he explained. "I'll send you copies of the rest as soon as I get home."

The sisters admired the different pictures, which showed the town and its people with uncanny accuracy and with a suggestion of great affection.

"These remind me of Norman Rockwell paintings," Louise said. "You have an excellent eye for composition and light, Ted."

"I couldn't wrap my gift," Max said, "but if you have a trash can, I can show it to you."

Mystified, Alice went and retrieved the small trash can from the office. Max thanked her and set it on the floor in front of him.

"This is really for Alice, but I think everyone here will appreciate it," he said.

Max removed a box of matches from his pocket and dropped them into the trash can. He then took out his cigar case and did the same with the cigars it contained. He paused, patted his jacket pockets and came up with a few more cigars and discarded those as well.

Everyone stared at the trash can, then at Max, in shock. All but Alice, who gently cleared her throat.

"Oh all right." After giving her one of his most ferocious scowls, Max sighed heavily and tossed his expensive leather case in on top of the cigars. "I quit. Happy holidays."

Everyone erupted into applause, and Alice insisted on giving the big businessman a hug. "I am so proud of you, Max Ziglar."

He returned the hug. "I'm also making breakfast," he said over Alice's shoulder. "French toast for the whole house."

A loud engine sound made Jane turn her head toward the windows. "What is that?"

Louise rose and went to look. "I believe it is a snow-plow, clearing the road."

Alice's mouth sagged open.

"Okay, I definitely believe in Santa Claus now," Jane said and grinned, "because that's exactly what I wanted for Christmas."

"You wanted your own snowplow?" Laura frowned.

"It doesn't look as if it is stopping here." Louise shaded her eyes with her hand. "Although there are two people coming up to our porch."

The two people turned out to be Aunt Ethel and a heavily dressed young man. Jane went out to greet them.

"How are you?" Jane walked up to the man and helped

him with his coat as if she knew him. "I'm so happy you could make it."

"I was stranded for a few days, but I talked the local road crew into letting me ride up here with them." The man removed his knit cap and the scarf covering the lower part of his face, which was covered with a neat black beard. Next he took off his sunglasses and looked across the room. He had very familiar, dark brown eyes. "Did he leave?"

"No." A pale Max Ziglar took a hesitant step forward. "I'm still here, John."

"This is Mr. Ziglar's son," Jane announced for everyone else's benefit.

Max, still staring at the younger man as if seeing a ghost, took another, hesitant step forward. "I can't believe it's you."

John Ziglar smiled and ran a hand over his beard. "I guess I've changed a little since the last time we saw each other."

"The last time I saw you, you were barely out of your teens. Now you've grown into a man." Max spoke as if in a dream and terribly afraid he would wake up. "I don't understand. How did you get here? How did you find me?"

"Ms. Howard actually found me. She called me last week and told me that you were visiting in this area." John Ziglar came forward, also quite slowly. "I wanted to get here over the weekend, but the weather changed that. It was pretty touch-and-go for a few days. I wasn't sure until late last night that I could get here."

"How in the world were you able to find him?" Alice murmured to her sister.

"I did a little research on the Internet," Jane whispered back. "I would have said something to you and Louise, but the storm hit, and I wasn't sure if John was still coming or if he had gone back home."

Max still seemed deeply shocked. "Why would you come here, John? Surely not for me."

The younger man glanced around the room. "This looks like a nice place, but there was no other reason I'd leave my family during the holidays and hitch a ride on a snowplow, except to see you."

"You did all that? Came through all this weather, to see me?" The businessman didn't sound as if he believed his son. "Why would you?"

John frowned a little. "You're my father."

"But I drove you away." Max's voice became strained and he looked at the floor. "I told you I never wanted to see you again."

The others tried to address their attention to the tree: This time was for the Ziglars.

"I know. I thought by now you might have changed your mind." His son's voice went low. "I've wanted to see you for a long time. I thought we should try to talk again."

That made Max stare at his son. "You mean that?"

"Yes. This seemed like a good opportunity. You know,

neutral ground for both of us." John Ziglar removed his glove and held out his hand, his expression still uncertain. "Merry Christmas, Dad."

For a long moment the businessman stared at the younger man's hand as if it might vanish. Then he looked into John's eyes and his own glittered with tears. "Merry Christmas, son."

Max ignored the outstretched hand and pulled John into his arms.

Dear Lord, forgive me for doubting You, Alice prayed silently. *And thank You for the snowplow.*

∽

Edwina excused herself for a moment and returned with a box of tissues, which she passed around to the other women. "I never thought I'd cry on a Christmas morning," she confessed as she blotted her tears. "But I haven't felt this moved since my son was born." She looked at Jane. "You've done such a wonderful thing."

Embarrassed, the youngest Howard sister shuffled her feet. "The effort was really all John's. He had to beat the weather and the traffic and the lack of transportation to get here. I only made some phone calls."

"I don't know many people who would care enough for a stranger to even think of something like this," Allan said, and took one of the tissues and applied it to his own watery eyes. When Edwina smiled at him, he shrugged. "My allergies."

"Mine must be flaring up too," Ted murmured as he reached for the box.

After the emotional reunion, Max took Jane to one side and clasped her hands in his. "I don't know what to say to you. I don't know how to tell you what this means to me or how to begin to thank you."

"I'm so happy for both of you." Jane smiled and squeezed his hands. "I'm also completely relieved that it was not a terrible mistake. I was worried that you might not . . ."

"Appreciate it?" Max grimaced and glanced over at John. "I don't blame you. I've allowed pride to steal too many years of happiness from me." He smiled, a wonderful smile. "Bless you for helping make this reunion happen for us."

Father and son had ten years to catch up on and they began to tackle the task over a Christmas Day breakfast of French toast, prepared by the sisters since Max was otherwise occupied.

"I have a studio in Manhattan now," John told his father. "I do graphic work, mostly advertising, but I've had a few shows in the Village and I'm starting to build a following. My wife Natalie is a sculptor."

"Your wife?" Max seemed taken aback. "You left a wife at home to come and see an old man?"

"Natalie has been encouraging me to see you for some time. She would have come with me, but her parents came down from Buffalo for a visit to see the boys."

Now Max looked staggered. "Your boys? You have children?"

"Twins." John took out his wallet and removed a family photo. "These are your grandsons, Dad. They'll be four in February. We named them Jason and Nathan."

The businessman took the photo with a trembling hand. "I have grandsons," he said, sounding utterly dazed as he focused on the picture. "Two four-year-old grandsons. We *do* have a lot to catch up on, John."

"My twin terrors," John said, his voice wry. "Nate is a sweetheart, like his mother, but Jason, Jason is a carbon copy of me." He grinned at his shaken father. "And you."

While their guests enjoyed the meal, the three sisters slipped out to the parlor to exchange gifts. Each was delighted by the others' thoughtful and appropriate presents.

Louise's last gift to Jane was the photograph she had taken from her school album and carefully framed.

"This is from your first Christmas with us," she explained. "I believe Father took this on Christmas Eve, after I'd gotten up to give you your bottle."

Jane studied the old black-and-white photo, which showed a teenage Louise sitting in an old rocking chair and holding a tiny, dark-haired baby against her heart. Both Louise and the baby were asleep, a bottle of formula resting on Louise's lap. Both faces were filled with peace.

"This is really me and you?"

Louise nodded. "I wanted you to know what got all of us through the year after Mother died. It was you, Jane. Taking care of you and watching you grow helped us to heal. We treasured you."

"How could we not? Look at the baby in that picture." Alice's voice grew soft. "You were so little and helpless, and yet you brought so much joy back into this house. Just as you do now."

Their sister seemed shaken. "I never looked at it that way."

"I have one more gift for you too. Thank heavens the power came back." Alice handed her a small wrapped box that contained an unmarked cassette tape, and plugged in a small tape player. "You have to listen to it."

"Did you record some of Louise's music for me?" Jane asked as she popped the tape in and pressed play. "Because I really like that Haydn—" she fell silent as a pleasant, mellow male voice began speaking.

"Praise the Lord, for bringing us together tonight."

"Oh, my Lord!" Jane went completely white and the baby photo fell from her fingers onto her lap. "Is that ... that's Dad."

"In a few hours it will be Christmas, brothers and sisters. This is the holiest of nights and it all began thousands of years ago, when some poor shepherds made an incredible discovery." Daniel Howard's voice grew rich with emotion and wonder. "They were given the news that a Savior was born unto mankind, a Savior who had brought love and hope back to the world."

Alice saw Jane reach out and take Louise's hand in hers.

"Can you imagine what it was for them, those shepherds in the fields, to look up and see the heavenly host praising the Lord? To learn that God loved us so much that he gave to us His only Son? Angels must have filled the entire sky. Light like nothing man had ever seen illuminated the world, for on this night God threw open the gates of heaven.

"On the night Christ was born, I believe it must have been like having heaven right here on earth. Until that moment, heaven had been beyond our reach, but now it was attainable. Those shepherds must have felt as if they could reach out and touch the face of God.

"In His infinite wisdom and boundless generosity, Almighty God sent to us His Son, Jesus Christ. That little baby, who would heal the lame and feed the hungry, who would become the Savior of all mankind, was His gift to us. Is it any wonder that God opened the heavens on this night when Christ was born? How else could you celebrate such a gift? Let us pray.

"Almighty Father, we thank You for this night and for the love You brought to our world through the birth of Your Son, Jesus Christ. Hear our joyful voices on this night and know that our hearts are Yours."

They listened to the rest of the service, until Daniel ended it with a loving reminder to his congregation.

"I hope that when you leave here today, you will remember that through you, Christ is heard, and that through your faith, someday the heavens will once more be opened and we will dwell in the house of the Lord forever. A blessed and happy Christmas to you all."

The tape stopped, the recorder clicked off and for a moment the three sisters sat in silence.

Finally Jane summoned up a single, dazed word. "How?"

"You talk in your sleep," Alice said. "You told me that what you wanted for Christmas was to hear his voice again."

Their youngest sister passed her hand over her eyes. "How did you find this?"

"Alice remembered that one year Fred Humbert recorded one of Father's Christmas Eve services," Louise replied. "We sent it to Aunt Ethel at her farm because she was too ill to visit us."

"I never thought…" Jane groped for words and then she looked at her sisters. "I am never going to be able to top this present. Ever." She glanced at the tape recorder. "May we listen to it again?"

Seeing the wonder and awe in her younger sister's eyes made Alice realize that the spirit of Christmas had never been more evident than it was on this day.

Pastor Thompson was right, she thought. *It is not the gifts that matter, but the love with which they are given.*